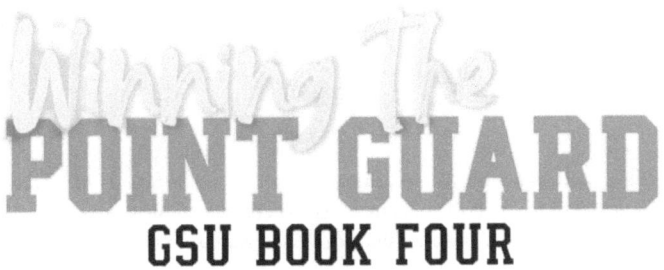

POINT GUARD

GSU BOOK FOUR

LAURA JOHN

Independently published.

Cover Designer: Brittany Franks with Chaotic Creatives

Editor: BreathlessLit

Proofreader: Crystal Clear Author Services

Sensitivity Readers: Darryl Bailey and Crystal Clear Author Services

DEAR READER,

This book has a few subjects that may not be easy for everyone to read so if you have any triggers please head over to my website for a full list of content warnings: https://www.authorlaurajohn.com/ winning-the-point-guard

CHAPTER ONE

SMILING faces pass me by as I make my way to my class. I can't believe this is my last year at Green Spring University. I've spent the past three years here working my ass off to be the best basketball player I could be while also getting my degree. My momma made me promise her that I'd graduate before declaring my eligibility for the NBA, and I'm on track to making my word true. If things go according to plan, I'll have my degree in hand, and my best friend and I will be signed to an NBA team by the end of June. Nine months to go.

"Yo, C, wait up," a familiar voice calls out, and I turn to see my best friend, Brendon, standing there with that permanent grin of his lighting up his deep, russet face. It's a look I've become accustomed to seeing, showing off his perfectly straight, bright white teeth. His ebony hair is styled in an artfully disheveled way, the kind that takes more effort to achieve than it would appear to. It's a stark contrast to the normal super short buzz he's worn in the past. But if I'm being honest with myself, longer hair really suits my best friend, making him even more handsome.

"Hey, B. How did breakfast with your parents go?" I check once he reaches up to me.

"Same as always," he replies with a shrug. "You'd think they would be sick of me by now and want nothing to do with me, but they still insisted on keeping our tradition of family breakfast for the first day of school."

I chuckle, shaking my head at him. "You know you're super lucky to have amazing parents like yours, right?"

He laughs and nods. "I know, but I really wanted to catch up with you this morning. I can't believe we spent the entire summer apart. I missed you, man."

This was the first summer we've ever spent apart. If life wasn't such a dumpster fire, we would have been together like normal, but instead I had to spend the entire time in Florida helping Momma clear out Grandma's house and settle her affairs. I thought it was going to be the most depressing summer ever, but it turned out to be better than I expected.

I missed my friends like crazy, but it was good for me to spend some time away. Over the past few months, I learned a lot about myself, and I'm not sure that would have been possible if I had stayed in my same routine.

Brendon and I met in kindergarten and became best friends by the second month of school. I still remember the day that he stood up to my bully for me and then declared we were now best friends. His lisp at the time made the declaration even better. Even at five years old, Brendon was a protector and problem solver, which is something I've always admired about him. Especially being more of a shy guy myself, at least around strangers. Once I've known someone for a while, I will come out of my shell and am a pretty outgoing person, but that doesn't happen overnight for me.

"I missed you too," I tell him as we walk down the hall to our class. "If your Instagram is anything to go by, you had a great summer."

Brendon's smile grows, and his amber eyes glimmer with joy. "It was killer! Although it totally would have been better with you around." He bumps his shoulder into mine, and I roll my eyes, but it's impossible to stop my grin. "How was your break? You went radio silent on the socials."

I lift my shoulders, trying to figure out how to answer him. We never went more than a few days without texting, so he already knows the majority of what went down, and now is not the time to share the things I've been keeping to myself.

"It was better than I thought it was going to be, but I didn't get up to anything crazy," I finally say as we get to our classroom.

"You didn't do *anything* other than what you told me in your texts?" he questions while we take our seats.

His intense stare causes my cheeks to burn as memories of my summer pop into my head. *A hot, warm, mouth marking kisses down my neck, my hands gripping tightly to the pale muscled arms beneath me.* Quickly, I turn away to rummage through my bag until I'm certain my face will no longer give away what I'm thinking about.

Brendon has no idea how loaded his question is and that's probably because I've never been known to keep a secret from him before. It's not like I'm purposefully withholding this from him. It's just I have no idea how to bring it up. I wasn't expecting my summer to be so eye-opening, and I'm nervous to retell exactly what went down.

"Did *you* do something crazy, and this is just your way of trying to even the playing field?" I counter, deflecting to the best of my ability.

Brendon throws his head back, laughing. The sound is loud and joy-filled, and it brings a smile to my lips. "There's only one thing I didn't tell you about, but it's more of a show than tell thing," he tells me, piquing my interest. "You'll have to wait until tonight to find out my secret." He winks at me, and I stick my tongue out at him like I'm five years old again.

I want to argue that I hate it when he keeps secrets from me, but how can I do that when I'm also withholding information?

Thankfully our professor starts the class at that moment, commanding our attention and allowing me a moment to forget about how awkward I feel. I'm going to have to tell Brendon *everything* that happened this summer sooner rather than later, or this anxiousness is going to eat me alive. Maybe we'll get a moment alone tonight. Then I'll be able to confess my secret.

CHAPTER TWO

CARTER IS ACTING WEIRD TODAY, and it's bothering me. Something is obviously up, but he isn't telling me what, which isn't like him at all. He's never kept a secret from me in all our years of being friends, so it doesn't make sense for him to start now, but he isn't acting like himself. The only time I've seen him be so awkward before is when he's around new people. But I'm his best friend, so why is he acting like this with me?

I wish I could force him to spit out just what the everloving fuck is going on already, but there hasn't been a single moment where we've been alone today, and it doesn't feel right to ask him to spill his guts around others.

Thankfully the day is almost over, and we'll have some time to ourselves soon. I just don't know if I'm going to call him out on his odd behavior or wait for him to tell me in his own time.

I'm normally a pretty patient guy, but I've never had to be around Carter before. He normally tells me everything the second it happens. Hence I'm more bothered by how he's acting today than I should be.

"Want to order pizza for supper?" I ask Carter once our class is over.

"Umm… yeah… sure… that should be fine," he responds,

stumbling over his words in such an awkward way that causes me to furrow my brows.

What the fuck is going on with my best friend?

Part of me wants to demand right here and now he tell me why the hell he's been acting like a weirdo all day, but the more logical side of me knows that would be mean. If he hasn't told me already, there has to be a reason, and maybe he'll feel more comfortable once we're by ourselves at home.

We make our way to Carter's car in silence, and even though my thoughts are focused on trying to figure out what is going on with my best friend, I can't help but feel like someone is watching me — a feeling I've gotten all summer. Casting a quick glance around, I don't see anyone with their eyes on me, so I shrug it off as usual then pull out my phone and place an order at our favorite pizza joint.

"Ham and pineapple good?" I tease as we arrive at his car, knowing how much my best friend loathes fruit on pizza. To my surprise, he nods, pursing his plump lips and running his hand over his short jet-black hair. He mumbles his acceptance of the pizza before opening his door and getting behind the wheel.

"Okay, that's enough," I tell him firmly once I've joined him inside.

"What?" Carter squeaks out, his dark brows shooting up and surprise dances behind his chestnut brown eyes at my random outburst.

"You've been acting weird all fucking day, and now you just agreed to pineapple on your pizza. Have you been abducted by aliens or something? Because this isn't you."

Carter shakes his head but won't look me in the eyes. "I don't know what you're talking about," he mumbles. "I've been acting the way I always do."

"Bullshit. Are you seriously going to act like I don't know you almost as well as I know myself?" I question him with a lifted brow.

Carter blows out a breath and hangs his head, running his fingers through the short strands at the same time. "There's just something going on in my head," he whispers, and I reach over to grab his shoulder.

"You know you can tell me anything," I remind him, and he nods his head once in agreement.

"I know that, but I'm having a hard time wrapping my head around this at the moment," he tells me. "It's not that I don't want to tell you, I'm just not sure *how* to right now."

I hate that he's keeping something from me, because I'm a fixer type of person. The last thing I want is to see my friends hurting, so if I can help in any way, I will. I'll be a listening ear or a problem solver if need be. However, sitting on the sidelines and letting people figure things out on their own has never been my strong suit. I do understand that sometimes it's difficult to talk about things. I just wish that wasn't the case right now. I guess I'll just have to be patient and accept that he'll talk to me about it eventually.

"Well, I'm here when you're ready," I assure him, squeezing his shoulder one last time before letting go.

He offers me a soft smile and nods. "I appreciate that."

Without another word, Carter starts the car, and we make our way to our favorite pizza joint. On the way, I stare out the window, lost in thought. It's times like this that I wish I was a mind reader, so I could help my best friend out without him having to find the words to whatever is troubling him. But this isn't a sci-fi movie, and as far as I know, being able to see into someone's thoughts isn't something anyone is able to do at this moment.

Hopefully, it won't take Carter too long to wrap his head around things and share with me what's going on because I really hate this awkwardness between the two of us right now.

CHAPTER THREE

THE TENSION that fills the air around me and my best friend as we eat our pizza is stifling, and I hate it.

I should have known trying to keep anything from him wouldn't work out for me. Brendon has always been able to see right through me like I'm made of glass or something. If I ever try to lie to him or hold back parts of the truth, he sniffs it out like a bloodhound on a hunt. Not that I've made a habit of lying to him or anyone else, really. I'm a shit liar. I don't even want to be withholding the information I currently am, but I wasn't lying when I told him I don't know how to tell him this secret.

How do you tell someone who has known you almost your whole life that you're not as straight as you once thought?

Over the summer, I met someone who helped me explore myself in ways I never knew I wanted, and it was literally life changing. I went from believing I was straight to fully embracing my bisexuality over the course of a couple of months.

I've always appreciated the physical appearance of both men and women. I wasn't afraid to say when I thought anyone was hot, and I've told plenty of my guy friends before just how sexy they are, never thinking twice about it. I thought everyone was like that. Maybe that's because I only had experience with straight relationships growing up, so I just automatically thought I was straight, too. I obviously wasn't gay because I *loved* being with women, but I never realized I was bisexual, either. That all changed this summer.

A memory knocks at the door of my subconsciousness, and I allow it to take me back to Florida.

THE AIR IS *hot and sticky as Mom and I pull up to Grandma's house and Mom takes in a shaky breath as she stares at the little home. The flower boxes that hang beneath the windows are overgrown with weeds, and what used to be white siding now has a yellow tinge to it. Grandma hadn't been well for a while, and it's obvious that she didn't have anyone looking after the place.*

I used to come here when I was younger. Grandma would always be waiting for us on the front porch in her rocking chair, with a giant grin and a plate of her famous chocolate chip cookies. Now, there's no one there, and the worn old chair looks as sad as I feel at this moment.

"Come on, we probably need to open the windows and air out the place so it isn't musty when we try to sleep tonight," Mom tells me. I nod before following her up the steps of the front porch, not worrying about our luggage at the moment.

It doesn't take us long to open the windows, and while Mom makes the beds, I get busy hauling in our stuff.

"You must be Ella's grandson," a man with dirty blond hair and a bright smile who looks to be around my age says as I'm pulling my suitcase out of the back of Mom's car.

I pause, set down my luggage, and nod. "I am. Did you know my grandma?" I check.

"I did. I've lived next door for the past three years and she kind of took me in under her wing. She was the nicest lady I've ever met," he tells me, making my heart ache for my grandma even more.

"She was great. I wish I could have spent more time with her. It

sucks that we lived so far away, and I only got a few summers and holidays here and there with her."

"Who's this?" Mom asks, coming out of the house to help me.

"I'm Henley," the man says, sticking his hand out to shake hers. "I am a neighbor and was a friend of your mom's. She was a wonderful woman, and if I can help you guys out with anything, please let me know."

Mom beams at him and nods. "I appreciate the offer. For now, I think we're okay, but I will let you know if there is anything we need."

He dips his chin then takes a step back. "I'm usually around, so just come knock on my door," he tells me before heading back to his place.

"Mom never told me she had such a nice young man living next door," Mom says, grabbing one of her suitcases and heading inside.

"I think she did mention a neighbor who was helping her with yard work," I reply, and mom nods.

"Now that you mention it, she did say something, I just wasn't expecting that person to be your age."

I shrug and follow her in with two suitcases in tow.

THE FIRST WEEK at Grandma's house is heavy with emotions. Going through all of her things has been stirring emotions inside of me that I wasn't expecting. By the time Friday hits, I'm beyond exhausted. Of course, my mom notices and tells me that I need to get out and have some fun. Apparently going to the gym to workout or the basketball court to practice isn't good enough. The last thing I want to do is go out to a bar by myself, but Mom thought of that too and asked Henley to take me out. I'd really rather not hang out with a stranger, but when Mom has something in her head, she sticks to her guns and refuses to relent.

Which is how I find myself getting into Henley's car on Friday night.

He's been over a couple of times throughout the week to check on us and I've learned a few things about him, but it's all surface level stuff like how he's an entrepreneur and runs his own business. It doesn't change the fact that he's still very much a stranger.

"You don't have to do this," I tell Henley after I've shut the passenger door of his car and close off my mother's ability to eavesdrop.

"I know I don't have to, but I want to," he assures me, flashing a wide, toothy grin my way. "Now, how exactly do you want to spend your evening?"

I shrug, casting my gaze downward taking in how clean this car is. There are no wrappers, discarded to go cups, or garbage like there normally is in my car. In fact, there's nothing at my feet at all, except the plastic liner that protects the carpet. I've never met anyone my age who is this tidy before.

"Do you like beer?" he checks, and I lift my shoulders again. Even though I actually hate beer, I can't bring myself to tell him that.

The small space is filled with my awkward energy, and I kick myself internally. Why do I have to be so odd around new people? Why can't I just let go and be myself?

"Do you like onion rings?" he inquires next, clearly refusing to stop his questions until I've given him something to go off of.

"I guess so," I reply quietly. "I mean, if you've tried one, you've tried them all, but I wouldn't say I hate them."

I glance at him quickly and notice how his whole face is lit up. His smile is almost too large for his face at the moment, but it doesn't take away from his handsomeness.

"I know of the perfect place to take you," he declares, finally putting his car into drive and taking off in what I assume is the direction of our destination.

I stay silent as Henley drives, looking out the window and taking in the beauty of Florida.

"You sure are a quiet guy," Henley notes out loud.

"I'm sorry," I murmur. "I get awkward around new people."

"Does alcohol help calm your nerves?" he asks, causing my lips to turn upward the smallest amount.

"It's been known to help on occasion," I reply, looking at him this time with a slight grin on my face.

Henley lets out a loud laugh, filling the space with his joy. This laughter helps ease some of my nervousness, which I'm grateful for.

"Well, good thing there isn't a shortage of booze where I'm taking you."

"Are you planning on getting me drunk just so I talk a little bit more?" I ask him with a teasing tone.

"Will it work?" he counters.

I shrug. "We'll just have to see, won't we?"

"I guess we will," Henley replies with a bright smile.

The rest of the drive is quiet but not as awkward as it had been when I first got in the car, and before I know it, we're parked in front of a rundown building.

I pull my brows together as I take in what's in front of me. The walls of the building are faded and chipped, probably not seeing any love or attention in many years. A neon sign hangs in a window that once upon a time spelt out beer in bright letters but half of them are burnt out now, leaving only the B and the second E to glow. I'm assuming this place is a bar, but it looks like a dump. Why did Henley bring me here?

"I know it looks like a shit hole, but I promise it's much better on the inside," Henley tells me, clearly having noticed my confusion.

I highly doubt that the inside could be that much better, but I decide to go inside with him anyway. If it turns out that Henley's lying, I can always turn right back around and order a rideshare back home.

Cautiously, I open the passenger door and follow Henley into the bar, which looks nothing like what I thought it would from the outside.

In my head I was picturing torn upholstery, dirty floors, and an *odor that would make my nose wrinkle, but I'm pleasantly surprised not to find that at all. Instead, the place is cozy, inviting, and clean. The hardwood flooring barely has a speck of dirt on it, and the large bar that sits just to the left of the front door is spotless, apart from the few drinks that are sitting on top of it. Edison lights hang from the ceiling giving the space a warm glow and makes me want to find a place to sit and just take in the atmosphere.*

"Told you it was better on the inside," Henley whispers with a smirk.

"And I one hundred percent doubted you," I reply, flashing my own grin at him. My words make him laugh and, thankfully, don't offend him.

"I could tell, but don't worry; you didn't hurt my feelings this time," he teases with a wink, then points his chin toward the booths that line the far wall. Why don't you get us a spot, and I'll order us some drinks?"

"How do you know I'll like what you order?" I question with a tilt of my head.

"I've been known to read people pretty well, but if you hate what I bring back, I'll get you something else," he assures me.

I don't see a point in arguing, so I make my way to an empty booth and sit down before looking around again.

The place is quiet, with only a few tables of patrons. It's possible that it's only like this because of how early in the evening it is. Or maybe people judge the outside like I did and don't give this place a shot. I'm busy studying two men who look to be in their sixties and are arguing over something, when Henley slides into the booth across from me. I give Henley a small smile but quickly cast my gaze back to the men, wishing I could make out exactly what they are bickering over. Even though they seem to be deep in debate they are both smiling, like they don't care that the other one disagrees with them. I don't think I've ever seen people argue so politely before. I mean, besides me and my best friend. We bicker all the time but never cross the line of taking things too far. Maybe these guys are best friends, too.

"That's Harold and Arnie," Henley supplies. I realize how rude I'm being and finally give him my full attention like he deserves. "They've been together for forty years. They fight constantly but love just as hard."

Okay, so obviously, those two aren't just friends. Now I feel a little weird mentally comparing them to Brendon and me.

"It looks like they enjoy arguing," I tell him, trying not to show my feelings.

He nods with a giant grin. "I think it's like a weird kind of fore-play for them. For as long as I've known them, they've been like that. But it's only little shit they disagree on. When it comes to the big matters of life, they are on the same page."

"I suppose that's good. And forty years is a long time to be together. It makes sense that they are going to argue from time to time, and if it adds a bit of a spark to their relationship, I don't see the harm in it."

Henley chuckles. "That's exactly how I see it. To be honest I'd count myself lucky if I found a partner that loved me as much as those two love each other."

I take note of how he said partner, and not boyfriend or girlfriend.

"So, you're a romantic?" I check while reaching for my drink, fighting the urge to wrinkle my nose when I see that it's beer.

I've never been a big beer guy, but I don't want to be rude, so I take a small sip. My brows immediately shoot up when a hint of fruitiness coats my tongue. I was for sure not expecting this to taste good. Maybe that's because I've only ever drank cheap beer at house parties that tasted like piss.

"It's good, isn't it?" Henley questions with a raised brow and a knowing smirk on his lips.

I shrug, trying to play it cool. "It's okay," I respond, making Henley throw his head back, laughing.

"You're a shit liar," he tells me, taking a sip of his own beer.

"Am not," I disagree, fake glaring at him, which only results in him laughing harder.

His laugh causes flutters to erupt in my stomach, completely catching me off guard. I've never had this feeling for a man before.

"Dude, do you not realize you wear your emotions on your face? You are so easy to read."

I huff out a breath but don't argue with him because others have told me that a few times. Sometimes, I hate being so transparent, but I also don't have the energy to change myself. It's not like it's a negative quality.

"Don't worry, it's cute," he assures me with a wink.

My face heats from the compliment, and I take another swig of my beer, hoping it will cool me off.

I should probably tell Henley I'm straight since I'm pretty sure he's flirting with me, but for some reason, I can't bring myself to say the words. And if I'm being honest with myself, the attention is nice, I just don't want to lead him on.

"Am I making you uncomfortable?" Henley checks, and I shake my head.

"No, but I should probably tell you I'm straight," I reply.

Henley doesn't seem taken aback by my response, but he tilts his head to the side, like he's studying me. "Does that mean you want me to stop flirting with you?"

I nibble on my lower lip, trying to come up with an answer. Do I want him to stop? I don't think I do. From the way my stomach is fluttering, I clearly have some sort of feelings for him, and I am really enjoying our time together. I definitely don't want the night to end. Maybe I should test the waters and see what it feels like to allow him to flirt with me.

I take a deep breath and slowly shake my head again.

Henley's smile grows in a devilish way. "Sounds good to me," he responds, his voice dipping an octave causing shivers to run up my spine. He never takes his eyes off me, not even when his tongue darts out to wet his lips. My eyes zero in on the action, making my new friend chuckle.

Tonight is definitely turning out to be something I wasn't expecting, but I can't say I hate it either.

THE EVENING IS FILLED *with laughter, light conversations, mouth watering food, a decent buzz from the beers, and a sexual tension you could cut with a knife, like when Henley got foam from his beer on his lips and licked it so slowly while holding eye contact with me. The hint of desire is so evident in his baby blues. Or when we kept brushing our fingers together whenever we reached for something on the table. The light touches ignite sparks inside me and have me sporting a half chub most of the night. I have never felt something like this before with a man, but it doesn't feel wrong.*

"You've never *seen Labyrinth?" Henley gasps after finding out I've never watched his favorite movie.*

I chuckle at his look of pure shock. "It came out before I was born."

"Same, but that didn't stop me from watching it. It's a cult classic, and I'm completely appalled that you haven't seen it. I'm pretty sure watching David Bowie in those tight pants is what brought on my bi-awakening. Of course, I didn't try anything with a guy until much later, but I'd confidently say that David Bowie was my first guy crush."

"Finding guys attractive doesn't make you bi," I counter.

Henley stares at me intently for a moment before responding. "Do you find guys attractive?" he checks with a quirked brow.

I shrug. "Doesn't everyone? I mean, a hot person is a hot person. Recognizing that doesn't instantly make you bi."

Does it?

"Okay, putting that conversation to the side, I still say it's a travesty that you haven't seen Labyrinth, and I think we need to rectify that as soon as possible," he states with a firm dip of his chin.

"Do you have an idea in mind to solve this dilemma?" I check, cocking my head to the side a little.

I hope he invites me over to his place because I don't want this night to end. And I'm curious to see how this will go.

Have I ever felt like this when hanging out with my other guy friends? Surely if I was actually bi I would have felt a pull toward other guys before. But maybe I didn't because no one ever came on to me before. Well, besides my dance coach but that always felt more like a joke than him actually wanting me. And I really thought I was straight, so what if I misread things thinking everyone felt like that?

Fuck my head is a mess right now.

"*I was thinking you could come back to my place and watch it with me. I feel like it's my duty to show you what you've been missing,*" *Henley says, pulling me from my thoughts.*

The way he's looking at me right now, with a lusty gaze and a sexy smirk on his lips, makes me wonder if his words have a double meaning.

My heart races and my cock starts to stir as my mind takes me down a dirty trail straight to the gutter.

That is for sure a first for me, but again I can't find it in me to care. I'm not homophobic and if it turns out I'm into guys and girls, I really don't give a fuck. But I do hope Henley's words earlier do have a double meaning, because suddenly I'd really like to explore with him and figure out how I'm feeling.

Holding eye contact with Henley, I swallow the rest of my beer and tilt my head. "*Come on, then. I'm excited to find out what I've been missing.*"

There is definitely a double meaning in my words. By the way Henley's smile grows, and his pupils dilate, I know he picked up on it.

Quickly we slide out of the booth and head over to the bar to settle our bill before leaving and making our way to his house for a night that I don't think I'll forget anytime soon.

I FEEL *like I'm about to crawl out of my skin as Henley pulls into his driveway.*

"Nothing has to happen if you don't want it to," Henley offers after putting the car into park and killing the engine. "We could just watch the movie, or you could even go home if you want. I'm pretty sure you were picking up on my other invitation, but if you're not ready for that, I won't be upset."

I nibble on my lower lip while trying to figure out what I want. I'm nervous as fuck, just like I was the first time I did anything with a girl, but there's also an undercurrent of excitement there too, and I don't want to shut things down just yet. I don't know how far I'll want to go tonight, but I do want to try something.

"I don't want to go home," I whisper.

Henley grins and tilts his head toward his house. "Okay then, let's go inside."

We both exit his car, and I follow behind him with an anxious, but eager energy coursing through my veins.

"Would you like anything to drink?" Henly asks once we're inside his house.

"A water would be nice," I reply while taking in the area around me.

The walls of the entryway and hall are light gray and are void of any decorations or pictures. They lack the personality I thought I would find in Henley's place. It isn't until I follow him into the living room that I find a space that suits Henley's personality.

"Have a seat and I'll get us some water," he tells me before heading into the kitchen.

I do as I'm told while also looking around the cozy room. It isn't overly decorated, but I have a feeling that the items that were chosen were done so with care and consideration. The walls are the same gray color as the hall, but there are a few pictures and some art work hanging on them, telling a story that I'd love to know. Who are the people that have earned the right to be show-cased? What is the meaning behind the painting that hangs beside the window? How hard did Henley have to work to receive the certificates that are on either side of his television? So many questions pop into my head as I take in everything that is surrounding me.

"I got that when my dad took me to my first baseball game," Henley tells me, seeing that my focus is currently on a baseball that is sitting in a plastic box in the middle of his coffee table. "We caught a foul ball, and we were able to get it signed after the game."

"That's so cool," I reply with a big smile and take the glass of water from his outstretched hand.

"I'm not the most sentimental guy, and I hate clutter but that is one thing I would never part with," he explains before grabbing the remote to que up the movie.

I guess we really are going to watch Labyrinth. Part of me kind of thought it was just a ploy to get me into his house, and maybe it was before Henley clued into how nervous I am. Obviously he wants more than to just watch the silly movie he's seen a hundred times, but he's also putting the ball in my court. He's letting me choose what I'm ready for, and when. I respect him a whole hell of a lot for that.

The movie starts and we fall into a comfortable silence as the scenes play on the screen. I can't help but smirk when I realize that Henley is mouthing the words along with the characters.

I find myself entranced by the movie and see why Henley's first crush was David Bowie. He's hot. Slowly I begin to relax, and I realize I'm leaning into Henley. His one arm is behind me on the couch, and his side is pressing into my arm. He doesn't push for us to get any closer, but he also isn't moving away. He's letting me set the pace.

I'm getting more and more comfortable as the movie goes on but feel completely thrown off when the characters start singing. I sit up suddenly and turn to stare at Henley.

"It's a musical?" I shriek, making Henley chuckle.

"You didn't know that?" he questions with a lifted brow.

"No," I reply, crossing my arms over my chest. "If I had known that I would have refused to watch it. I've always hated musicals."

"Well, so far you've seemed to really like this one. Why don't you at least give it a chance?"

I glare at him for a moment, but his arms seem rather inviting and I really was enjoying the movie so, fuck it. I move back into position but this time I actually snuggle into him and smile when his hand drops to my upper arm. I've never been held like this before, but I'm already enjoying it.

By the time the movie ends I'm pretty happy that Henley made me watch it, because even though it was a musical, it was great. But as the credits roll, I wonder what we should do now. I could obviously go home, but I don't want to do that. What I think I really want to do is kiss the man holding me, but I'm also nervous to ask for it.

Slowly, I twist in his arms and place my hand on his chest.

"So, what did you think of it?" he asks, rubbing my arm at the same time.

"It was okay," I murmur, but my smile gives me away.

"Just okay, hmm?" he questions then tickles my side.

I laugh and squirm as his fingers dig into my side. Without realizing it, we move into a position where I'm lying down, and Henley is hovering over me. His touch turns gentle, and a shiver runs up my spine. My laughs are cut short as I take in a sharp breath.

"Would it be okay if I kissed you?" he questions, his fingers running up and down my side.

My mouth turns dry, and I find it impossible to speak, so I nod my head and close my eyes as I wait for his lips to touch mine. The nerves and excitement running through my veins make my heart beat faster. I really want this, but I know things are going to change as soon as this happens.

It feels like forever before Henley finally kisses me, but when he does it's like the room starts to spin. I'm suddenly dizzy with lust and desire, and I immediately cling to him. My hands roam up and down his back as his lips move against mine.

Kissing a man is nothing like kissing a woman, but that doesn't make it one better or worse, just different. I feel the exact same *amount of euphoria that I do when making out with a woman, but I obviously also know that it isn't the same.*

Henley's body is all hard and toned and his stubble rubs against my face giving me a small amount of beard burn that I surprisingly love. His erection presses firmly into my leg and my own cock pushes against the confines of my jeans and underwear, begging to be touched.

"Want. More," I murmur against his lips as I try to unbutton Henley's jeans.

"EARTH TO CARTER," Brendon says, pulling me from my daydream.

I shake my head and clear my throat, trying to calm my racing heart. How the hell did I let myself fall that far down memory lane while sitting in front of my best friend?

"Sorry," I murmur before grabbing my glass of water and downing it.

"You completely zoned out on me," my best friend states, staring at me with concern written all over his face. "Are you alright?"

I wave him off and fake a laugh. "I'm fine. Just got lost in thought. But now I gotta piss. Be back in a minute," I tell him before excusing myself and making a beeline for the bathroom.

Once the door is shut behind me, I lean against it and throw my head back.

"Fuck," I whisper under my breathe.

If I'm going to keep daydreaming about my time with Henley, I'm gonna have to tell Brendon about my summer or things are going to become even more awkward.

CHAPTER FOUR

Brendon

I STARE at Carter's empty chair, utterly confused as to what just happened. I noticed my best friend starting to space out half-way through his second piece of pizza but when he completely went off into la-la land I started to get concerned. It's not like Carter to daydream when we're having dinner together, and I was a little nervous that maybe something serious was happening. Thankfully it wasn't anything bad, but I'm still baffled as to what is going on.

Most of me wants to respect Carter's need for space but there is also a small part of me that wants to force him to talk to me. What the hell is he keeping to himself that is causing him to act so off? Did something bad happen to him this summer?

My thoughts start to take me down a dark path and I shudder at the possibility that my best friend was hurt in an unimaginable way.

"I'm sorry for being weird," Carter murmurs when he comes back to our small dining area that we use for both eating and studying.

"You know you can tell me anything, and I would never judge you," I reassure him. He nods slowly but keeps his gaze on the table.

"I know that, but something happened this summer, and I

don't know how to tell you," he whispers while fiddling with his thumbs.

A lump forms in my throat as my fear feels like it's becoming a reality.

"No matter what happened I'll always be here. Nothing will stop me from being your best friend."

"I met someone," he tells me and finally lifts his eyes toward mine. "They completely turned my world upside down, and I can't stop thinking about them."

I stare at him intently trying to figure out if he was hurt or if he just had a summer fling and he's still hung up on this girl.

"In a good way or a bad way?" I question, needing to put my mind at ease.

"Good way," he assures me and the knot in my stomach instantly releases.

"So, you're acting like a weirdo because of a summer fling?" I double check.

"Kind of, I guess," he mumbles, and I can't help but laugh.

"Dude, that isn't a big deal at all. Are you like in love with this chick or something?"

He shakes his head. "No, it was just a summer fling. Neither of us was looking for something long term. We both knew it was only going to be for the couple of months that I was in Florida. Besides, I'm not ready for a real relationship anyway. But I wasn't with a girl this summer. I was with a man…"

It takes a moment for his words to register with me, but it leaves me even more confused as to why he didn't tell me this sooner. Does he think I'm homophobic or something?

"So, let me get this straight. You've been acting like a completely different person all day because you had a summer fling with a guy?" I ask and he nods slowly. "You know I don't care who you sleep with."

Carter blows out a breath and slumps into his chair a little. "I know that deep down, but it just felt like a big deal. Like for as long as you've known me you've always thought I was straight and now I'm not. I wasn't sure how you would take it."

"Dude, you know I don't give two shits about stuff like that. Love is love and lust is lust. All I care about is that you're happy. Did this guy make you happy this summer?"

I might be straight, but I totally don't care that my best friend is coming out to me. I'm just happy he's happy.

The tips of Carter's ears turn a deep shade of red and he nods as a dopey smile spreads across his lips. "Really fucking happy," he mumbles, and I laugh.

"Then we're good. Now stop acting like a fucking crazy person and be my best friend again," I scold him with a wide grin so he knows I'm not actually angry at him.

"It's really that simple for you, isn't it?" he asks me, and I nod.

"Does that surprise you?" I counter.

He shakes his head and shrugs. "Actually, no. I should have known that you would be just like me and not freak out. I thought I was a little weird at first when I didn't panic over being with a guy, but it felt right, so I figured, what's the point in freaking out? I guess being bi actually makes more sense to me than being straight, but honestly, the label doesn't really matter to me either."

"Okay, now that you realize that I'm not going to judge you or act weird, let's move into the living room so you can tell me about this guy," I tell him, standing up and heading to the sofa.

Carter chuckles as he follows behind me.

"What do you want to know?" he asks as he gets comfortable on the recliner.

"Anything and everything. By that stupid grin on your face earlier, you clearly had a good time, and I want to know if this guy is going to turn into something special at some point."

"His name is Henley," Carter starts. "And he was my grandma's neighbor. He owns his own business and is a cool guy. He took me out for drinks my first weekend there and opened my eyes to the fact that I'm not as straight as I thought. I guess I just assumed that I was straight because I had never been with a guy, but after he explained that sexuality is a spectrum and not all black and white, everything just started to make sense. He offered to help me explore anything I wanted, and we had a great summer together. At first, I felt bad because I knew he was a romantic deep down, but he assured me that he knew better than to get his heart involved. So, we had a summer fling, and the rest is kind of history."

"Your summer sounds so much cooler than mine," I murmur, making my best friend laugh.

"Oh, come on. From all the texts you were sending me, it sounded like you had a blast. And what was that surprise you wanted to show me?"

An excited energy courses through my veins, and I practically jump up and race to my bedroom, grabbing the stash my cousin gave to me.

"Cancel anything you have planned for this weekend and don't add anything new to your calendar," I tell him, holding up the baggie of premium weed. "We're getting lit my friend."

Carter starts cackling and almost falls out of his chair as his laughter takes over his body. "How come I am not surprised at all that your big surprise is a bag of pot," he tells me with glassy eyes.

"It's not just any pot," I argue. "It's high-quality weed from my cousin's company."

He snorts a little and nods while wiping away the few tears that have started to fall. "Of course it is. Well, good thing I don't have plans for this weekend. You can count me in for a good time."

I lift my fist and cheer. "Fuck yeah!"

I'm beyond excited to have a fantastic weekend with my best friend. Thankfully, the awkwardness is behind us, and we can move as we always do.

CHAPTER FIVE

THE IMMENSE RELIEF I felt after telling Brendon that I'm bi was like nothing I had ever experienced before. I was wound so tight, and I really didn't have any reason to be. Brendon reacted exactly how I would have expected him to if I wasn't so caught up in my head.

With the confession off my chest, we were able to move forward without any more awkward tension, which I was beyond grateful for. I know it was only one day of weirdness, but it was enough to make me feel like I was in a parallel universe. So, to be back to normal is everything I could have wanted and more.

And thankfully, I slept like a baby last night, which probably wouldn't have been possible had I still been trying to keep my secret.

Brendon and I are sitting at the table eating our breakfast when the front door flies open. Our other best friend and roommate comes hobbling in on a pair of crutches.

"What's up, losers?" Artie asks with a big grin.

He's followed by his parents who are carrying his stuff. His Dad nods at us then darts down the hall to drop the stuff he's carrying off in Artie's room, while his mom makes her way to the kitchen to put away the groceries she's carrying.

"Yo, A!" Brendon cheers and throws a plushie basketball

in his direction. "I thought you were going to be missing the whole first week of school?"

Artie can't get his hands up in time, so he takes the soft ball to the face and laughs as it bounces off and lands on the floor.

"Way to hit a guy when he's down," Artie teases, inching his way into the place. "And yeah, I was supposed to have the week off but one of my professors this semester is a dickwad."

"Language, Arthur," Artie's mom scolds him as she rejoins him by the door. Both Brendon and I press our lips together to stop ourselves from snickering.

"Sorry," Artie mutters before continuing his story. "Anyway, he said he didn't think I deserved special treatment, and if I wasn't in his class to receive the entire course load, then I'd automatically flunk."

"Fu-," I'm about to curse but Artie's mom shoots me a glare and I stop myself, mouthing an apology to her. "You broke your leg three days ago and he won't give you a break?"

"One class isn't going to kill him," Artie's dad says while walking over to his wife and son. "He has to take it easy, but he's completely capable of being at school. He's lucky he got the majority of his classes off this week."

"Do make sure he takes it easy, though," his mom adds. "No crazy activities and absolutely no drinking."

Brendon and I look at each other, sharing a silent conversation with our eyes that basically says, *I won't tell if you don't tell.*

"We'll make sure he behaves, Mrs. Miller," Brendon assures her, even though I know he means no such thing.

Brendon is all for going hard and pushing every limit. He doesn't know the definition of behave. The fact that he hasn't gotten into more trouble with the school surprises the shit out of me. He's always been the instigator of our little *A, B, C* group.

Artie's mom knows all about Brendon's shenanigans and shakes her head sighing. "Maybe I should get a hotel room for the week so I can keep an eye on you."

"Mooommm," Artie groans. "I already told you I'll be fine. You have to stop treating me like a baby."

"Heather," Artie's dad says in a calming tone while wrapping an arm around his wife's shoulder. "He's a big boy and can take care of himself. I'm sure he won't do anything stupid."

"I'd believe you if he didn't just jump off a cliff and break his leg," Arite's mom grumbles at her husband.

"Everyone was doing it, and I was the only one that got hurt," Artie says as if that helps his case.

"And Izzy was watching so he couldn't chicken out," Brendon adds with a shit eating smirk.

"Not helping," Artie growls out at him.

I press my lips together and keep my mouth shut, not needing to get involved. But that doesn't mean I'm going to disappear into my room either. I'm all for some good drama as long as I'm not in the middle of it.

Artie's mom sighs again and presses her fingers to her forehead. "Okay, we need to leave before I regret allowing Artie to come back on his own."

"I promise I'll be on my best behavior, Mom," Artie assures her as she pulls him in for a tight hug.

"I highly doubt that, but I guess at some point I have to let you make mistakes and learn from them. Just please don't kill yourself," she pleads with her son, and he snickers but nods.

"That's an easy promise," he tells her then kisses her cheek.

"Don't be an idiot," his dad tells him, then adds, "again."

"I'll be taking it easy for at least a couple of weeks," Artie replies with a grin.

"The lord really did want to test me with you," Artie's mom mumbles before allowing her husband to pull her out of the apartment.

"Gosh, my mom can be overbearing sometimes," Artie grumbles as he hobbles into the living room.

"All moms are like that," I remind him.

"I know, but it can be exhausting sometimes. Especially when you're a dumbass and injure yourself, resulting in so much babying it could drive even the biggest Momma's Boy crazy."

I chuckle. "Well, if you would have let go of the rope swing when you should have, you wouldn't be in this situation."

I wasn't there when Artie got injured, but I heard *all* about it.

"I was distracted," Artie whines.

"By Izzy's big tits?" Brendon checks with a smirk.

"Fuck off," Artie grumbles grabbing another basketball stuffie from the couch beside him and hurling it at Brendon who catches it easily, cackling the entire time.

"You're so easy to rile up man," Brendon teases. "But in all seriousness, I'm sorry you got hurt."

Artie nods. "Thanks, I appreciate that. But you're not wrong. Izzy is the reason I was distracted. I was trying to show off. Now she probably thinks I'm a loser."

Artie has been crushing on Izzy since he met her freshman year. She's a cute cheerleader and exactly his type. However, she had a boyfriend then, so Artie didn't have a chance. But Izzy and her boyfriend broke up at the end of last school year and Artie planned to woo her over the summer. Obviously, things didn't end on a high note for him, but that doesn't mean she's written him off just yet.

"Did she call you a loser to your face?" Brendon asks with a lifted brow.

Artie rolls his eyes then slowly shakes his head. "She's not a bitch so she would never say it to my face. But who wouldn't think I was a loser for breaking my fucking leg like that?"

Artie's phone pings at that moment and his brows shoot up when he unlocks the screen. "Well, shit," he whispers before looking up. "Apparently, Izzy doesn't think I'm a loser and wants to hang out this weekend."

I can't help but laugh. "See, you were all worried for nothing."

"You can't hang out with her this weekend. I got premium weed from my cousin. We were supposed to smoke," Brendon tells him, looking like a kicked puppy.

"Dude, you know I love you like a brother, but I would *much* rather hang out with a hottie than smoke weed with you two idiots."

Brendon huffs out a breath then nods. "I guess when you put it that way it makes more sense. And that just means it's more weed for me and C."

"You know I'm a lightweight and I'm only going to take a couple puffs," I remind him.

"We'll see about that," he retorts, and I sigh.

I've never really been able to tell Brendon no before. Something tells me this weekend might end up being crazier than I thought it was going to be.

CHAPTER
SIX

Brendon

THE WEEK FLIES by in a mixture of classes, study sessions, and meetings with my coaches and personal trainers. The team will start practicing together soon, in the meantime it's about making sure everyone is on the right track. Since I didn't slack off over the summer there isn't much I have to change, but that isn't the same for everyone.

Something that has become a new normal for me is having this constant feeling of being watched. It started over the summer and hasn't stopped. Sometimes I feel like I'm going crazy because even though I feel like someone is spying on me when I look around no one is ever there, or at least no one of suspicion.

By the time Friday hits I'm beyond ready to let loose.

"You sure you don't want to bail on Izzy and hang out with your boys instead?" I tease as Artie hobbles toward the front door.

"Absolutely not," he replies, quickly, without even thinking about it, which is rude, but understandable. I mean if I had my eye on a girl, I wouldn't let him dissuade me from hanging out with her. "She even told me her roommate is out of town for the weekend and I could crash in her room if I wanted to, so don't be waiting up."

"I'd wish you all the luck getting into her pants, but

you're probably not even allowed to have sex right now, are you?"

Artie tips his head from side to side. "Doc said no strenuous activities, but I don't think having Izzy sit on my face is too strenuous."

I laugh and wish him all the best as he leaves with Carter who agreed to give him a ride since he can't drive for a while.

While they're gone, I have a quick shower and place an order for some greasy burgers. I make sure to order double what we normally get since we're guaranteed to get the munchies later. I also made sure to stock up on snacks earlier, so we're all set.

"THANKS, MAN," Carter says to who I'm assuming is the delivery guy as I'm walking down the hall. I make sure to keep my steps light as I attempt to sneak up on my best friend. He shuts the door and yells, "Food's here," before realizing I'm already behind him.

"Smells good," I whisper, causing him to jump and almost drop our food.

I double over, laughing so hard my sides hurt.

"Dude, you got some serious air there," I tease him once I'm able to breathe properly again.

"You're an asshole," he grumbles, stomping toward the kitchen table.

"Maybe, but you still love me," I counter.

"That's debatable sometimes," he argues while looking into the bag that holds our dinner. The hint of a smirk on his lips lets me know he isn't actually pissed at me, which is good. It's never my goal to actually make him mad. "Why'd you order so much?"

"In case we get the munchies later," I tell him as I push his hand to the side to grab myself a burger.

"Good thinking," he concedes while grabbing his own burger.

We both sit down at the same time and start to dig in.

"Fuuucckk," I moan around my mouthful. "These are sooo good."

Carter starts to cough and choke at that moment, and I rush to get him a glass of water.

"Dude, are you going to die?" I ask as I pat his back and pass him the glass.

He shakes his head and pushes my hand off before gulping down the water. "I'm fine," he mumbles once he can talk again. "I guess I just forgot how to eat."

I chuckle as I sit back down, thankful that he is okay and not needing to go to the hospital.

I pick up my burger and start to eat again, only moaning a little this time. I forgot just how good these burgers are. I definitely should have pigged out on them a little more this summer.

Carter clears his throat and drinks some more water down, and I study him closely to make sure he's actually okay. If I *have* to take him to the doctor I will. The last thing I want is for him to actually die. He's my best friend and life would seriously suck without him.

The tops of Carter's ear are a deep red, the color they always turn when he's embarrassed.

"You good, C?" I check, hating that he's self-conscious about his little choking episode.

He nods, keeping his eyes on the table. "I'm good, just had a little something still stuck in my throat. I'm gonna get some more water."

As he fills his cup, I finish the rest of my burger and sit back, tapping on my flat stomach. "That was some good food."

Carter gets back and shakes his head, but when he looks at me his brows pull together, and he sucks his lower lip between his teeth. It's the look he's always gotten when he was confused, but I don't know why he would feel like that right now.

"You good?" I ask him again and he blinks a couple times before nodding and putting on a smile.

"Yeah, man. I think choking just threw me for a loop is all."

"Makes sense. You did almost die," I tease and shoot him a wink.

He chuckles dryly in response, but it sounds forced and the tips of his ears turn red again. Is he blushing from my wink?

I internally shake my head. He's probably just still embarrassed about choking the way he did. I've winked at him a million times before and it never caused him to blush.

"I'm gonna roll a joint and get a movie queued up while you finish eating," I tell him and his shoulders relax, lowering a little, almost like he's relieved I'm leaving, which is weird, but I don't feel like thinking about it too much right now. "Make sure to take your time," I remind him before heading to my room to grab the baggie of weed and some rolling papers.

Hopefully the rest of the night is uneventful and filled with the happiness only a good high can bring.

CHAPTER SEVEN

I'M SUCH A FUCKING IDIOT.

Who the hell pops a boner from the moans of their straight best friend? Then gets scared from said reaction and ends up choking on their food.

I'm such a fucking idiot.

Thankfully Brendon was none the wiser at everything that was happening to me internally, but I couldn't help feeling a bit of relief when he left me alone for a few minutes.

Brendon has always been someone who enjoys food, letting everyone know with the noises he makes while he eats. I've never once felt aroused by said noises before. How come my body decided that tonight would be a good time to change things up?

Maybe it's because it reminded me so much of the moans Henley would make when I was sucking him dry. My cock probably just doesn't know the difference between the two noises.

No need to panic.

At least I hope there's no need to panic. The last fucking thing I need is to start becoming attracted to my best friend.

The moans confusing my cock make sense. What doesn't make sense is how my heart started to beat a little faster as I watched Brendon rub his bare stomach.

It was obvious that Brendon had just showered from the

way his hair was still damp, and a few droplets of water clung to his chest. He was only in a pair of gray sweatpants and at that time, I thought nothing of it. That's what Brendon normally wears when he's chilling at home.

However, my body was beginning to have a different reaction to him after my choking incident.

Get your shit together, C. We cannot be affected like this by B. He's our best friend and we will not *jeopardize this friendship,* I internally scold myself.

I take a deep breath while Brendon is still in his room, trying to center myself. I'm sure the way I'm feeling is just a chain reaction and everything will go back to normal now that he isn't moaning. The rest of the night is going to be like it always is and I won't think of my best friend in a lusty way.

If I keep saying that to myself enough times, hopefully it will come true.

"What should we watch?" Brendon calls out and I get up to toss the rest of my burger in the garbage. I'm not hungry anymore.

"Something stupid and funny," I reply as I join him in the living room and plop down on the couch.

"It's like you read my mind," Brendon says, shooting me a big grin before turning his attention back to the streaming service.

He scrolls for a while and I relax, watching him from time to time as he comments on each movie that he passes. I don't pop another boner and I don't feel a random pull to him like I did earlier, and that has me feeling instantly relieved.

See, I didn't have anything to be worried about. I'll just have to be careful eating around him, which isn't a big deal. At least I'm not into my best friend.

"Fucking perfect," Brendon says as he selects the movie and I shake my head while smiling.

We've both seen *Van Wilder* a million times, but it's also kind of the perfect movie to watch high.

"Ready to have a good time?" Brendon asks, holding up the joint and lighter.

"Ready as I'll ever be," I reply dryly, trying to suppress my smile and sound bored.

Brendon gives my shoulder a shove as he sits beside me. "Don't act like you aren't excited. You might pretend to be a wet blanket sometimes, but we both know you like letting loose as much as I do."

I shrug, refusing to admit anything.

Brendon rolls his eyes before lighting up the joint and taking a hit. "Your turn loser," he says, passing the joint to me.

I take a deep inhale, savoring the feel before slowly blowing out the smoke then passing the joint back.

Brendon's cousin is a master at growing weed and this shit really is premium quality. It's not skunky and won't make you gag and cough each time you take a hit.

We both take a couple drags before snubbing it out and starting the movie.

It doesn't take long for my body to start to feel like Jell-O and for all my worries to fade away. The movie is funnier than I remember, and I find myself laughing at every little stupid thing. Brendon of course is doing the exact same, shoving me on the parts that crack him up the most.

When a couple of the characters start having sex on the screen, Brendon tilts his head to the side, knocking into mine, and I wince, rubbing the sore spot.

He chuckles and holds up his hands when I glare at him. "Sorry," he apologizes quickly. "I was just studying the girl. She's hot, but like not as hot as this one chick I saw in a porno over the summer."

I blink at him, trying to figure out where he's going with this.

"What's your favorite kind of porn?" he asks, cocking his head to the side as he studies me with cloudy eyes.

Fuck, he's so high. I mean, so am I, but I'm not randomly bringing up porn. But nonetheless, I think about his question and answer it.

"I've never thought about this before," I tell him as I ponder over the kind of porn I've watched recently. "I normally just scroll until I find something I like."

Brendon nods along in understanding. "Yeah, but what do you like?"

I shrug. "Not gonna lie. The ones that have the really stupid intros always pull me in."

He laughs. "You mean like, *my stepsister got stuck in the dryer and the only way to help her out was to fuck her and use her cum to set her free?*"

I snicker and nod.

"Dude," Brendon says with wide eyes, staring at me intently. "We should watch porn right now."

I blink rapidly and shake my head, clearly I heard him wrong. "What did you just say?"

Brendon's already picking up the remote as he responds. "I said we should watch porn. We've seen this movie a million times already so it's not like we need to finish it."

I'm frozen in place as I stare at him, and he pulls up a porn site. Are we seriously going to do this?

There's a part inside of me screaming for me to tell him no. To walk away. That this is a horrible idea and can only end one way. While another part of me, that part that seems to be winning tells me to stay. To see what's going to happen.

Brendon's cackle pulls me from my daze, and I turn my attention to the television.

Tears are streaming down his face as he tries to read the title of the porno. "I slipped and fell on my stepdad's cock," Brendon barely manages to get the words out before doubling over.

His laughter is contagious, and the humor seems to wash

away my fear, and I begin to laugh along then read the next title. "I ordered a pizza, and it came with a side of dick."

Brendon almost falls off the couch as his laughter takes over his body and tears of my own start streaming down my face as I laugh at him.

He continues to scroll and stops at the best title yet. "I went to the gym to get fit and only ended up fittin' this dick in my mouth," Brendon reads, and I laugh hard before telling him to put it on.

Neither of us is apparently paying close attention to the thumbnail; that or Brendon doesn't care, but I'm caught off guard when the video starts, and it's two dudes.

I expect Brendon to shut it off, but he doesn't. Instead he leans back against the couch and starts to rub his crotch as he listens to the lame lines the guys are spewing.

Why isn't he shutting it off? As far as I know, Brendon is as straight as an arrow. Is he simply doing this for me, since he now knows I'm bi?

My heart is racing so fast I almost feel lightheaded and even though I know I should, I can't take my eyes off my best friend.

"Relax, C. It's not a big deal," Brendon says with an easy smile as he slides down his sweats enough to free his cock, which is *massive*.

I've seen it a time or two, since he's never been shy about nudity and likes to change wherever he wants. But I've never seen it hard, and never like this.

I gulp down the lump that's forming in my throat but move to lean back like Brendon is doing and slowly unzip my jeans. My cock is already rock hard, and when I pull it out of the confines of my pants, there is an instant relief.

Keeping my eyes glued to the screen so Brendon doesn't think I'm jacking off to him instead of the porno, I begin to stroke myself.

"That's it, C," Brendon encourages me. "We're just two

guys watching porn and jacking off. Nothing wrong with that, right?"

Since I'm unable to respond verbally, I simply nod my head in response.

Yeah, this isn't a big deal. There's nothing wrong with what we're doing. This doesn't have to change anything.

I'm leaking precum like a fucking sieve, so I pull back my foreskin and swipe my thumb over the tip to use it as lube since I don't want to dry stroke my cock. While keeping my focus on the guys on the screen, I hear Brendon spit, and a shiver runs down my spine. Why is that so hot?

I try to keep my breathing even, but I'm already so close to blowing—not from the video, but from the idea of doing this with my best friend. I want to look at him so bad, to see what his face looks like when he comes. But that feels like it would be crossing a line. Jacking off next to each other is one thing; watching each other come is an entirely different thing.

One of the macho guys on the television is kneeling in front of the other, letting his partner drive his fat cock down his throat, and the sight makes my mouth water.

Memories of sucking Henley off pop into my head but quickly morph into a fantasy, and instead of my grandma's neighbor, it's Brendan feeding me his cock. It's like the thought has the power to push me over the edge, and I gasp as ropes of cum start shooting from my pulsing cock.

"Fuck," I breathe out as my entire body vibrates from the intensity of the orgasm.

"Jesusssss," Brendon hisses out, and I assume he's also coming, but I don't dare look.

Things are already fucked, at least on my end, and I don't need my best friend knowing what really made me come as hard as I did. That's a secret I'll have to learn to keep. Because if he knew the truth, our friendship would be over.

CHAPTER EIGHT

Brendon

I FEEL like I'm floating as I lean against the couch with my softening cock still in my hand. The mixture of the high from the weed and the fantastic orgasm I just had is otherworldly. And it hasn't passed me by that one of the most intense orgasms of my life happened while watching gay porn while sitting next to my best friend.

I guess this confirms that I'm not as straight as I once thought.

Carter has talked a lot about discovering his bisexuality this summer over the past week and the things he learned about the fluidity of sexuality. To say that he had the wheels in my brain turning would be an understatement. I have experienced more than a few things that he was talking about, which confused me more than I care to admit, but I didn't really want to think too much about it at the time. The conversations we had weren't meant to be about me, so I kept my internal thoughts to myself and let my friend tell me everything he was feeling.

I ended up doing a lot of research on my own after we went to our own rooms and began questioning so many things. Similar to Carter, I grew up only surrounded by straight relationships until I got to college. I was asked which girl I was crushing on at school, never which *person*. And even now that I have a lot of gay friends, I don't think I have a single friend, besides Carter now, that has told me they're bisexual. Since I *do* like girls, I just automatically thought that made me straight.

Looking back on growing up through a new lens, things definitely seem to make more sense if I consider myself bisexual. I'm pretty sure I've had a crush on a guy or two, but since I thought I was straight, I just assumed I really liked them as friends.

Take Carter, for example. I think I started crushing on him when I was about ten. I've always hated it when he had a girlfriend, but I figured it was simply because he was spending less time with me. I didn't realize that it was actually jealousy.

And even though he kept his focus solely on the television while jerking off, I was watching him the entire time. Taking in the small glimmer of gorgeous copper skin that was on display as he stroked his perfect uncut cock. Enamored by the obscene amount of precum he produced and the panting moans he made as his fist glided over the deeper chestnut shade of his engorged and glistening crown.

My mouth literally watered as I watched him and I was desperate to touch him, to taste him. But just because he's bisexual doesn't mean he's attracted to me, and I didn't want to put our friendship in jeopardy. It was already a big risk doing what we did. And for the life of me, I'm not sure why I did it.

I could blame it on the weed making me horny, which is partially true. It definitely lowered my inhibitions and was why I suggested watching porn in the first place. But choosing a gay one was all me. I wanted to see how Carter would react to it. I wanted to see if he would get as turned on as I was.

I was anxious at first that I made the wrong decision when Carter tensed up at the suggestion and completely froze when I pulled out my cock, but for some reason, I didn't stop. I could have royally fucked up everything I cherish the most, but I just continued to go with the flow.

Thankfully I was able to calm him down and convince him this wasn't a big deal, even though it was to me. Once he leaned back and pulled out his perfect dick, I damn near let out a sigh of relief.

"I'm going to go clean up," Carter murmurs, pulling me out of my haze, and I nod.

"Let me know when you're done," I reply, wishing we had more than one bathroom right about now.

He dips his chin before heading down the hall, and I grab the remote to shut the porn off. There's really no point in continuing to watch it since I've already came. But once the room is silent, panic starts to creep its way, tightening my chest and making it hard to catch my breath.

What the fuck did I just do?

My heart races so fast I'm afraid it's about to beat its way out of my chest.

What if this changes everything between us and I lose my best friend?

I can't lose Carter. He's my everything. My ride or die. My other half.

I might not have realized I was crushing on him until just the other day, but that doesn't change the fact that he's always been one of the most important people in my life.

Fuck! At this point, I wish I never would have figured out that I was bisexual. At least then, I could have continued to believe I just had an overly attached friendship with him. But now that I know the truth, everything has changed for me. I just don't think it's changed for Carter.

Maybe I can just pretend like nothing has changed.

As far as my best friend is concerned, the movie and the weed made me horny and think about porn and nothing more.

"Dude, put your cock away. The jerk-off session is over,"

Carter says, pulling me from my downward spiral. I turn to look at him, shoving my dick into my sweats at the same time.

His eyes lock with mine and I swear I see a hint of something new behind those alluring chestnut brown orbs, but maybe I'm just projecting. As we silently stare at each other, I take a moment to really study his face. Have I ever realized just how fucking handsome he is before? Sure, I knew he was an attractive dude, but he's absolutely breathtaking. Short jet black hair that's always styled perfectly, rich brown skin without a single blemish, eyes that suck you in if you let them, and thick, plump lips that would look perfect wrapped around my cock.

We stare at each other for way longer than anyone would consider normal before he blinks and shakes his head like he just came out of a daze.

"The bathroom is all yours. I'm going to bed. I'll see you in the morning," he mutters. Before I have time to respond, he's already gone, leaving me alone with my thoughts once again.

The way Carter stared at me was different from how he'd looked at me in the past. There was something new there; I just don't know what it is.

A small part of me is hopeful that it was attraction, and maybe he's also figuring out that his feelings aren't purely friendship based. But a larger part of me fears that the look was different because he hates what we just did. I have no idea what I'm going to do if it's the latter.

CHAPTER NINE

MY BODY IS desperate for sleep, but my brain won't shut down and give it to me. It's too fixated on reliving every single moment from tonight.

The main image that keeps popping into my head is the way Brendon stared at me when I told him the bathroom was free. It was like he was enamored by me or something. And unless I was only seeing what I wanted to, there was a hunger in his gorgeous amber eyes. It stole my breath and I allowed myself to get lost in his gaze for far longer than I should have.

The second I was able to shake myself out of my daze I said goodnight and bolted to my room, praying that he didn't see how much he was affecting me.

Why the hell am I suddenly affected by Brendon like this? Even though I've always thought he was hot, I've never popped a boner for him before. I've never had shivers run down my spine when he looked at me. And he sure as hell has never stolen my breath.

Maybe that's because I never saw Brendon as an option. As far as I knew, we were both straight, so all I felt toward him was friendship. Of course, I always wanted to be around him, and his hugs made me feel better than anyone else's, but I thought that was normal for best friends.

As I stare at the ceiling, I start to reevaluate our entire friendship.

People have made comments about our friendship in the past, saying how we acted more like husbands than best friends, but we just laughed them off. Yeah, we might be a little codependent on each other, but that's just because we are that close.

At least that's what I always thought.

Maybe there's a deeper reason why I want to spend all my time with him, and I just haven't been able to see it until now.

It would explain why I always struggled when he dated someone. I may have been missing my time with him on a level much deeper than mere friendship.

Having feelings more than friendship would also explain why I always felt more at ease when he was by my side or how his smile could make my whole day better, why his touch always calmed me, and why I dreaded spending a summer away from him.

Even though I was hooking up with Henley, my thoughts drifted to Brendon often, not in a sexual way, but just in a way that he was never far from my mind. When I thought about him being with a girl, I would call Henley and ask him if he wanted to mess around. That alone should have tipped me off that my feelings for Brendon weren't entirely platonic, but I didn't put two and two together.

It's like I had blinders on when it came to my best friend. Now that they're off, I see everything in a new light, which terrifies me. Just because I have feelings for Brendon doesn't mean he feels the same way, and the last thing I want is to ruin our friendship. I'd rather just push down these new thoughts than risk spending a life without the guy who makes me feel whole.

Wait. What?

I mean, he does make me feel whole, but dammit, how am I just coming to this conclusion now?

I blow out a breath and cover my face with my hand.

I kind of wish I never figured out I was bi this summer,

because now I have a feeling everything is about to blow up, and it's going to fucking suck.

ONLY GOD KNOWS what time I managed to actually fall asleep. By the way my body aches and my eyes feel like sandpaper, it's evident the small amount of *zzz's* I managed to catch weren't restful in the slightest.

The low hum of deep bass passing through my door is possibly what woke me up. Either that or my thoughts, which didn't stop even in my sleep.

As I become more alert, the sound becomes clearer, and I recognize the song that's playing. A small smile pulls at the corners of my lips as Brendon's favorite song plays. An image of him dancing in the kitchen pops into my head, but instead of just laughing and thinking that he's an adorable goof like I normally do, I start to get turned on.

I groan and grab my pillow from behind my head and place it over my face to stifle my frustrated shout.

Once I'm done letting out my irritation, I toss the pillow to the side and try to figure out what to do.

Should I talk to Brendon and let him know what's going on with me?

No. That's probably the dumbest idea I've ever had.

But am I a good enough actor to pretend like nothing has changed?

A knock on my door prevents me from fully spiraling and I turn my head toward it as it slowly opens.

"Oh good, you're awake," Brendon says with a bright smile, but it slips from his face and his brows pull together as he stares at something. "Why is your pillow on the floor?"

I shrug, trying to play dumb. "Must have had a restless

sleep." The fact that I do often have restless nights makes my lie believable.

"Shit, that sucks. But I know one way to make it better," he tells me, waggling his brows then pausing for dramatic effect like he often does before finishing his sentence. "Pancakes."

"Are you still high?" I question with a raised brow and a smirk.

Brendon throws his head back as he laughs, and I'm drawn to how carefree he looks. He doesn't look as stressed out as I feel right now, which is kind of annoying. Was he really not affected by anything that happened last night?

"Not high anymore, just love pancakes," he replies with his signature grin that I've grown to love and crave over the years.

I find it hard to respond at first because my emotions are at an all-time high right now, and I don't want Brendon to know that. If nothing has changed for him, he can never know that my feelings for him are morphing.

After clearing my throat, I finally manage to get some words out. "How you are able to stay in such great shape with your obsession with pancakes is beyond me," I mutter.

"You know I put the time in at the gym," Brendon replies flexing his muscles. The sight has tingles of desire coursing through my body shooting directly to my cock.

I quickly shift and reach for my pillow that's on the ground, throwing it at my best friend, so he leaves and doesn't see my arousal.

"You're a fucking idiot," I tease, trying to keep my voice even. "Now leave me alone so I can get dressed. I'll be out in a couple minutes."

"Don't take too long or I'll be back with a handful of ice. That's a sure fire way to wake you up," Brendon jokes with laughter in his voice before walking down the hall and finally leaving me alone.

I throw my head back on my mattress and breathe out a frustrated sigh. Things are going to be so awkward, and I have no idea what to do about it.

CHAPTER TEN

Brendon

WHEN CARTER COMES out of his room, he looks beyond exhausted. His feet shuffle across the floor and he looks like he barely got a wink of sleep. My heart hurts for my best friend and I internally vow to make his day better in any way I can.

"Extra strawberries and a dollop of whipped cream," I say as I set his plate on the table. "Just the way you like it."

Carter stares at the table, pausing in his tracks for a moment before giving his head a little shake and taking his seat. "Thanks. It looks great."

I study him for a moment, hating how he's acting so strange. Is he regretting what we did last night? Or is he just extremely tired? He does get like this from time to time. He's struggled with insomnia for almost as long as I've known him, and nothing has ever helped, at least not without major side effects. So, he's just learned to deal with the bad days to the best of his ability. And I try to help as much as I can, too.

"I've also made coffee. Let me get you some," I say, moving to doctor up his cup the way he likes.

I pour a large amount of honey into the bottom of a mug before filling it up halfway with coffee and the other half with milk. I have no idea how he drinks it so sweet, but he's been drinking his coffee this way since he started drinking the stuff. He used to use sugar at one point in time, but ever since he discovered honey in his coffee, he refuses to go back. Apparently, it makes *all* the difference. I remember one time we ran out of honey, so I used sugar instead, and I thought he was going to kill me for the change. I made sure to always have a surplus of honey from that day forward. A pissed off, uncaffeinated Carter is not someone you want to mess with.

"Here you go, stupidly sweet just the way you like it," I say, setting his coffee down and taking my seat beside him where my food is already waiting.

"Says the man who drowns his pancakes in ungodly amounts of syrup," he responds with a little smirk.

I smile in return, thankful that he seems to be getting back to himself.

"I still don't understand how you don't like maple syrup," I say before taking a bite of my pancake that's a tiny bit cold now but still fucking delicious.

"I'll admit real maple syrup is much better than cheap table syrup, but for some reason, I still don't like it on my pancakes. Strawberries are much better," he states before taking a big bite.

My eyes lower to his lips wrapped around his fork and my cock starts to stir in my sweats. When his tongue darts out to lick his lips, cleaning up the whipped cream that was there, I have to stop myself from groaning. I'm positive he's not purposefully trying to be sexual, he's just eating like he normally does, but today it's turning me on.

Apparently, I'm staring for too long because Carter squirms a little and reaches for a napkin. "Do I have something on my face?" he asks, patting his lips, and I have to swallow down the ball that is lodged in my throat as I shake my head.

"No, you got it. Sorry, I just zoned out," I lie, feeling like a douche.

I need to admit that things changed for me last night, but I have no idea how to bring it up without the potential of destroying our friendship. I've developed an attraction to a friend before. All the girls I've dated or hooked up with were either acquaintances or random chicks I met at a party. Never someone I was close with. That could mainly be because I don't have any close friends who are girls, but it doesn't change the fact that this is a first for me.

And it's not just any friend, it's my *best* friend. The guy who is always there for me. The one who I turn to for everything. The person who I never want to live without.

"Are you sure?" Carter checks. "You had this weird look in your eyes that I've never seen before."

Now would be the perfect time to come clean and lay my cards out there for him, praying that he feels the same way.

I take a shaky breath ready to take the plunge when the front door opens and Artie hobbles in.

"You're home early," Carter says as our friend makes his way over to us.

"I could smell the pancakes all the way at Izzy's house and just had to come get me some," Artie says while pulling out a chair and taking a seat. "But also, it's noon, my guy. Did you guys have such a crazy night that you forgot how to tell time?"

"He couldn't sleep," I supply.

"Shit," Artie says with a grimace, knowing all about Carter's insomnia. "I'm sorry about that. Did you have lots of episodes over summer break, or has it been a while?"

Carter thinks about it for a moment, and I get up to dish Artie up a plate, not bothering to make it special like I did for C.

"Actually, I don't think I had an episode all summer," Carter says, sounding shocked at the realization.

"That has to be a record for you," Artie notes. "Did you start a new medication or something?"

Carter presses his lips together and shakes his head as I'm

setting Artie's plate down, and I notice his ears turning a dark shade of red.

"No, but I was kind of sort of hooking up with someone all summer. Maybe orgasms are the trick to no insomnia episodes," Carter states.

I want to argue that statement can't be true because he orgasmed last night, but I don't want to out Carter to Artie. And also, because last night was special to me and I don't want to share those details with anyone.

"Orgasms are miracles, I swear. Like I wouldn't be surprised to find out my leg is miraculously healed already," Artie says, and I can't help but snicker.

"Is that your way of telling us that you and Izzy got it on last night?" I check and he flips me the bird.

"A gentleman never tells."

"What's stopping you then, because you're definitely not a gentleman," Carter teases.

Artie rolls his eyes and throws his head back with a sigh. "How did you two become my best friends when you're both such assholes?"

"You love us, don't lie," I respond, tossing him a wink.

"I thought I did, but I think I'm changing my mind," he grumbles.

"Tough shit, you're stuck with us," Carter tells him. "A, B, C for life."

The corners of Artie's lips twitch upward before a full-blown grin breaks free. "Fine, I guess I can continue to put up with the two of you."

We all laugh and eat more of our pancakes.

"So, what did you guys get up to last night?" Artie asks as I'm taking a bite, and I start to choke as memories flood to the surface.

Carter quickly moves to smack my back and I reach for my coffee to wash down the food that's lodged in my throat. I cough like a man who's been smoking cigarettes for his entire life, gasping for air when I can. Thankfully my airway doesn't fully get blocked off and the food eventually makes its way down, finally allowing me to catch a full breath.

"Look who's having trouble eating today," Carter notes with a mischievous smirk.

I narrow my eyes at him because he knows exactly why I choked at Artie's question, and he's acting like the same dirty thoughts didn't pop into his head.

"Dude, are you okay?" Artie asks and I wave him off.

"I'm fine. I think it's just karma's way of getting back at me for laughing when Carter choked on his food last night," I murmur before taking another sip of my coffee.

"To answer your earlier question, we got high and watched some movies. It was pretty uneventful," Carter tells Artie.

Fuck. How can he play it off so cool when my insides are literally in knots right now?

"Sounds like my night was waaay more entertaining," Artie responds looking smug.

If only he knew the truth.

"You keep bragging about that, but now I'm wondering if it was only good for you. Should we call Izzy and ask for her opinion on the evening?" I ask with my head cocked to one side and a shit eating grin on my lips.

Artie's face quickly turns into a glare and if I didn't know him as well as I do, it might have actually scared me. "If you embarrass her like that, I'll rip your fucking head off." He damn near growls the words out, throwing me off guard.

I was expecting to rile him up, but I didn't see him becoming this pissed off at my goodhearted teasing.

"Shittt," Carter says, drawing the word out. "You really like her, don't you?"

I nod along since Carter just said exactly what I was thinking.

The anger leaves our friend being replaced with a flus-

tered insecurity. He rolls his eyes and lets out a self-depre-
cating laugh as his cheeks turn from their naturally pale color
to a bright pink.

"What makes you think that?" he questions, fidgeting
with the hem of his shirt.

"By the way you're acting," Carter replies with a gentle
tone. "I've never seen you get so fired up over a dumb joke."

"Your blush when Carter mentioned it is also a dead give-
away," I add.

Artie blows out a breath, throwing his head back in the
process. "It's fucking stupid," he murmurs. "We haven't even
had an official date and I'm already crazy about her. Only
crazy people act like that, right?"

I shrug. "Falling for someone isn't something we can
control. Neither is how they make us feel." My eyes track
their way to Carter who's biting his lip and staring at the
floor, like he's purposefully trying to avoid my gaze. Does he
know my words are about him? Not wanting Artie to clue
into *my* feelings, I quickly tear my eyes away from Carter and
look back at my other friend. "Izzy seems like a nice girl so I
can see why you are crazy about her already."

"But we haven't even been on a real date yet," Artie
argues.

"You don't have to date someone to fall in love with
them," Carter says softly and my heart races.

Is it possible he's talking about me right now? Or is he
thinking about his summer fling? Fuck, I really wish I had the
ability to read minds right now.

"I guess that's true, but I'm still not used to crushing on a
girl this hard," Artie replies, having no idea about my internal
crisis at the moment. "And after hanging out with her one on
one, I'm even more into her."

"Did you ask her out on a date?" Carter asks and I try to
push away my thoughts so I can stay in the moment.

Artie's smile grows and he nods. "Yeah. We're going out next weekend."

"That's awesome man," I tell him with my own grin. "Fingers crossed she likes you just as much. Although, if she's really a smart girl, she'll run now."

Artie laughs at my joke this time and flips me the bird, letting me know he's not offended.

"As much as I'd love to continue to make fun of you, I've got homework I need to get done so I'll see you losers later," I state as I stand and clear the empty plates from the table, placing them in the sink for one of us to deal with later.

"Mind if I join you?" Carter asks, and I nod because it would be weird of me to tell him no, but at the same time, an alarm goes off in the back of my head, telling me that this is a bad idea.

I guess only time will tell because I can't take back my acceptance now.

CHAPTER ELEVEN

WHY THE HELL did I invite myself to study with Brendon?

I should be creating some distance between us until I can control my feelings. Of course, that's not what my heart wants, though, and that's what took over my mouth earlier.

I'm seriously considering just telling Brendon how I feel so that we can move on. Yes, things will be different after, but things are already changing, and at least with my feelings out in the air, we can figure out how to deal with them.

A teeny tiny part of me is hoping that Brendon will also have feelings for me, but that's like wishing for a unicorn, it's not going to happen. A larger part of me just prays he won't care and will let me down gently. At least then I can mend my heart and we can find a new way to be friends. I won't even let my brain go down the worst-case scenario road because it's too devastating.

I take a moment to wash all the dishes before joining Brendon in his room. I mean it's the least I can do since he made us breakfast.

With my books and computer in tow, I gently knock on my best friend's partially open door, pushing it the rest of the way once he invites me in.

My heart beats faster as I take Brendon in. He's sitting crisscross on his bed with a pile of books, his laptop beside him, and a pencil in his mouth. How someone makes a pair of sweatpants and a hoodie look sexy, I have no idea, but Brendon is pulling it off. I'm slightly torn between being thankful he has a shirt on, and wishing he didn't at the same time.

"Ready to get your homework done?" he asks, the corners of his lips turning upward but there is a hint of apprehension behind his amber eyes.

I share the feeling with him, but it's not like I can turn around now. I simply nod, since I can't find words and sit in front of him, toward the end of his bed.

"I'm really glad this is our last year of college," I say as I'm flipping through my notebook to find what exactly I'm supposed to be working on.

Brendon nods with understanding written all over his face. "Dude, same. I mean I love all our friends here, and GSU is a fucking kick ass university, but I'm over the studying. I'm ready to just play basketball."

I chuckle because those are my exact feelings, too. "Are we the same person?" I tease.

Brendon's deep laugh wraps around me like a warm hug, and I realize that the feelings he evokes from me aren't new, I just didn't fully understand them before. I had put them in a different box and justified them as something they probably never were. Of course, that has all changed now that I realize I like him as more than just a friend.

"We aren't the same person, but we're close enough to think the same," Brendon eventually says with a bright toothy grin.

I smile back at him before we both fall into a peaceful quiet as we start to tackle our work.

We both reposition ourselves from time to time as our bodies get tired of being in one position for too long. At one point, I scoot up the bed, thinking I'm about to lean against the headboard, but I don't realize Brendon has moved behind me, and I fall into his chest.

"Shit," I gasp out, sitting up quickly. "I didn't realize you were there."

Brendon chuckles and shrugs. "You can lean against me if you want," he suggests. "I'm just reading some chapters at the moment."

"That's not weird?" I question, trying to refrain from nibbling on my lower lip.

He shrugs it off casually while shaking his head. "It's not to me."

I take a deep breath through my nose before slowly blowing it out, staring at Brendon the entire time.

"My bed's a little small for us to be shoulder to shoulder anyway," he tells me while stretching out his legs, inviting me to sit between them. "This way we both have something to lean against while we read."

My heart and my brain are at war as I try to decide what to do. A week ago, I probably wouldn't have thought twice about this. Yes, it seems intimate, but we've always been close, and I would have played it off as something bros do. But things are different now, and I wonder if this is crossing a line, especially since he doesn't know about my feelings for him.

"I mean, if it makes you more comfortable, I can just scoot over and we can try to make it work," Brendon offers but I shake my head.

"Nah, it's cool," I finally respond, moving into position.

As I rest my back against my best friend's chest it becomes hard to breathe, and I try not to panic but this feels like too much. Honestly, it feels *too* perfect. My heart sighs, loving every moment of this even if it isn't an actual embrace, it becomes hard to breathe, and I try not to panic, but this feels like too much. Honestly, it feels *too* perfect. My heart sighs, loving every moment of this, even if it isn't an actual embrace. But that's why it's dangerous. To Brendon, this is nothing more than two friends studying together, and to me, it's everything. But that's why it's dangerous because to Brendon this is nothing more than two friends studying together and to me it's much much more.

"Are you okay?" Brendon asks, probably noticing how stiff my spine is at the moment. He gently runs his fingers up and down my arm, which causes goosebumps to erupt over my skin.

I shake my head, finding it hard to come up with words. Now would be the perfect time to tell him how I'm feeling. I know shit could hit the fan, but I'm not sure I care anymore. I need to get this off my chest. Fuck the consequences.

"I need to tell you something," I whisper.

Brendon squeezes my arm and sets his book down. "You can tell me anything. You should know that by now, C."

I nod, thankful that he can't see my face right now.

"But what if what I'm about to say changes everything?" I question, nibbling on my lip, unable to stop myself this time.

"Is change always a bad thing?" he asks, running his fingers over my arm again.

"It's scary," I reply.

"You don't have to be scared with me, C. Nothing you ever do or say will push me away. I'm always going to be here. No matter what," he assures me.

"I think I like you as more than just a friend," I confess softly and Brendon's hand freezes on my arm.

A shiver runs down my spine and panic begins to set in. Shit. I fucked this up. I shouldn't have confessed my feelings. I should have just kept this to myself. I'm going to lose the one person who means the most to me because I couldn't keep my fucking mouth shut. Everything is going to change.

My stomach curdles as I realize what I'm about to lose.

"You're not shitting me right now, are you?" he checks, giving me the opportunity to lie if I want to, but I can't do that to him.

"I'd never joke about something like this," I tell him, turning slightly in his arms to look at his face.

"Thank fuck," he breathes out, and before I have time to comprehend what's happening, his lips are on mine.

My eyes bulge out as my best friend's mouth moves against mine in a gentle kiss, wondering if I'm possibly dreaming this up. When his tongue whispers against the seam of my lips, seeking entrance, I close my eyes and allow this to happen, even if it most likely is a hallucination.

When I part my lips, Brendon's tongue dips into my mouth, tangling with my own and causing a tiny moan to ripple up my throat. I should be embarrassed by how needy I sound, but I'm too drunk on his kiss to care.

Strong hands grip my hips and move me so that I'm straddling my best friend as the kiss turns more heated and frantic. I grind into his lap and my eyes roll into the back of my head as I feel Brendon's hard cock pressing into me.

"Fuck yeah," Brendon whispers against my lips when I rock into him again, causing me to freeze.

This isn't a fucking dream or a hallucination. It's real, and now I'm panicking.

I try to scramble off my best friend's lap, but he refuses to let me go.

"What's wrong?" he questions with furrowed brows and slight frown. "Did I cross a line?"

I shake my head quickly, my heart pounding so hard it's making me lightheaded. "No, I'm just confused," I tell him honestly. "How is this happening right now? You're straight."

Brendon chuckles and lifts a shoulder. "Turns out you weren't the only one to figure out you weren't as straight as you once thought."

I blink at him a few times, struggling to fully understand his words.

Thankfully he doesn't wait for me to say anything before continuing. "When you were telling me about the things you learned over the summer, about sexuality and the varying degrees of it all, I started to do my own research and ponder my own sexuality. After a couple of days of web browsing, and thinking back on life growing up, I realized that straight isn't the best label for me. I'm bi, like you, and I think I've had a crush on you for a long fucking time."

I stare at him with wide eyes for a moment not fully believing what I just heard.

"Are you shitting me?" I whisper, echoing his words from earlier.

Brendon's smile is soft as he slowly shakes his head. "I'd never lie about something like this. I like you, C. As more than just my friend. And if you really feel the same way, like you said you did, then I want us to give this a chance."

"What if it fucks up our friendship?" I ask with a tilt of my head.

"I think it's worth the risk," he confesses. "Because now that I know we both have feelings for each other, it's going to be really fucking hard to go back to just being friends. I want more, and I want it with you."

I bite my lower lip both ecstatic and petrified that this is happening.

"And if something happens and we aren't meant to be partners, then we just go back to being friends. We both know plenty of people who have dated and are now friends. It doesn't have to be the end for us," he assures me.

"And you're positive you want me?" I question, hearing the wobble in my voice.

Brendon lifts his hand to caress my cheek and I can't help but lean into his touch. "There is no one else I want."

I was right earlier in thinking everything was about to change, but I was wrong about which way they were going to go. I don't have to worry about losing him anymore. Instead, we get to take things in a brand new direction. We get to explore this together and I couldn't be happier.

Slowly I stick my tongue out to wet my lips before nodding. "Okay."

Brendon's entire face lights up at my response. "Are you fucking serious right now?"

I chuckle this time and nod again. "I'm serious. Let's give this a shot, but I think we should take things slow. This is too important to rush."

"Whatever you want," he tells me before giving me a quick peck that has me smiling from ear to ear.

"I can't believe this is happening," I murmur while shaking my head.

"Believe it, C," Brendon replies with a wide grin. "Doesn't it feel right, though?"

I take a deep breath, pausing before I respond while reflecting.

Brendon has always been my person and it really does feel right that this is the turn our friendship is taking. In some ways, this was inevitable. Like the universe always wanted this for us, it just waited for us to realize what was directly in front of our faces.

"It feels more than right," I respond before leaning in to kiss him gently.

"Okay, now get back into position so we can finish our studying," Brendon says, giving my thigh a playful swat.

I laugh and move so that I'm back between his legs, leaning against his chest, but this time, I'm not stiff as a board. I relax into his hold.

"That's better," Brendon whispers, then kisses the top of my head and I nearly melt.

Brendon's free hand rests on my hip as we both pick up our books and start reading again.

I don't think I've ever felt as at ease as I do in this moment.

Who would have thought that one summer would change everything for us, and for the better.

CHAPTER TWELVE
Brendon

IT'S impossible to wipe the smile off my face as I read the textbook. I'm not *fully* taking in what I'm reading as I'm more focused on how good Carter feels in my arms, but I can't bring myself to care.

How has so much changed in such a short amount of time? Just yesterday Carter was only my best friend, and I knew I loved him, but it wasn't like this. This is everything I ever could have wanted and never knew I needed.

Things seem so easy right now, but is it always going to be like this? Eventually, we are going to have to come out to our friends and family, and even though I think they'll be happy for us, it's still going to be a huge adjustment for everyone. Not to mention that we'll eventually face homophobia at some point because that is just the world we live in, and what's that going to do to Carter? I have thick skin and could care less about what people have to say about me, but C is different. He takes words to heart, and it would gut me to know that he's hurting because some narrow-minded dipshit felt the urge to hurl insults at us just for being with each other.

"You okay?" Carter asks, picking up on my discomfort.

"Just thinking about the future," I tell him, putting my book down before running my fingers up and down his arm.

"What about it?" he questions, moving in my arms so that I'm still holding him but can see his face.

"I guess the unknown is a little scary," I tell him honestly. "We're going to have to come out to our friends and family, and, eventually, the public."

"Did you want to keep this a secret?" he asks with furrowed brows, worry oozing out of him as I shake my head.

"No, I just don't want to see you hurt if someone rejects us for being together."

His features soften, and the corners of his lips turn upward. "I know that not every person on this earth is going to agree with our relationship, but they don't matter to me. Our family and friends do matter to me, but I find it highly unlikely that they'll be disapproving of us."

I nod. "I was thinking the same thing. Are you wanting to come out publicly or keep our relationship to those closest to us?"

"I think we should keep it to just our friends, family, and teammates for now," he suggests. "The problem with coming out publicly is that it could affect our chances of getting drafted." I sigh, hating that we have to even think about this shit, but Carter must take it as me being upset with what he just said because he rushes to continue his thought. "It's not that I'm ashamed of you. I'd love to tell everyone about us but you know how the world can be."

I squeeze his arms and smile at him softly. "I completely understand what you're saying. I was only sighing because it sucks that we live in a world where we have to think about these things and can't just love who we want to love. I think keeping our relationship on the down low for a while is a smart idea. What do you think our coaches are going to think of us being in a relationship?" I check as the thought pops into my head.

Carter presses his lips together and his dark brows pull together once more. "Honestly, I think they'll be okay with it, but we should tell them before the season starts. It's best to have them on our side in case we face any backlash if people do find out about us. And I'd like for us to tell the team at our first practice. Obviously we know most of the guys well enough, but if there is someone who is secretly homophobic, having the coaches backing us will make a big difference."

My smile grows and I can't help but stare at him in awe. "Fuck, you're so smart," I muse out loud making Carter's ears turn that deep redish color. "So besides the coaches, our team, our family, and our friends, is there anyone else we need to tell?"

The color drains from his face, causing me to become worried. "What just popped into your head?"

"Our fucking sponsor deals have morality clauses," he grumbles and I see where he's going with this.

"Is there something in them about us not being able to be together?" I question.

Carter nibbles his lower lip as he shrugs. "I don't know. But we both know that we can't really afford to live in this apartment without those deals."

Carter and I both have endorsement deals with companies that pay us to represent their brands, and it's literally the only way we are able to afford all of our expenses without having real jobs this year. GSU only recently started allowing college athletes to make money off their names, images, and likenesses, and it's been a game changer.

If we both have to get regular jobs again, it could seriously fuck up everything that we've worked so hard for. It would put a tremendous amount of strain on the both of us and could affect how we play. If we can't play to the best of our ability, we could get benched, and our dreams of being NBA players could go up in smoke.

The absolute last thing I want is to have to hide my feelings for Carter, but I also refuse to put his future at risk. If we have to keep this strictly between the two of us to keep our deals in place, then that's what we are going to have to do.

"I could ask Sasha to read over our contracts and see what exactly the morality clause states," Carter suggests, mentioning his old dance teacher who was also a law student at GSU.

"That's not a bad idea," I tell him. "But do you think he'll have questions about *why* you are wanting to know this information?"

Carter shrugs. "Probably. But I know he would keep our secret if I told him."

I nod, knowing that Sasha is close with Carter and would never out his friend. "Ask him. The sooner we know the answers, the better."

He offers me a small smile before grabbing his phone and sending off a text.

"Okay, now we wait," Carter says, and I pull him in for a hug.

"I *really* don't want to keep my feelings for you a secret, but I'll understand if we have to."

"It won't be for too long. Once we sign to an NBA team, we'll be able to come out," he assures me before pressing his lips to mine.

Neither of us talks about the strong possibility of us getting signed to separate teams. I think that's because we don't want to put that idea out into the universe. If we simply keep saying we'll be on the same team, maybe that will make it a reality one day. One can hope anyway.

Carter's phone vibrates as we kiss, and he quickly moves to check the text message.

"Sasha says he's more than happy to comb over our contracts," he tells me with a big grin. "But he also wants to meet for an early dinner so I can spill the tea."

I chuckle because even though I don't know Sasha well, that sounds exactly like the guy I've met a couple of times.

"Go have fun with your friend. Just make sure he knows how important it is to keep our secret until we have answers."

Carter nods before giving me a quick kiss. "I want to have a quick shower before I meet up with him," he tells me as he removes himself from my embrace.

I kind of wish I didn't have to let him go. He feels so fucking perfect in my arms.

"Wanna watch a movie in here after your dinner?" I check and the smile that he shoots me warms my heart.

"Sounds perfect to me."

He winks at me before leaving my room and the giant grin that's on my face almost hurts, but I really don't care.

Things are good right now, and hopefully the morality clauses in our contracts aren't anything to worry about.

CHAPTER THIRTEEN

I'M GRINNING like a damn fool as I pull up to the restaurant Sasha wanted to meet at. I know that there are still a lot of things up in the air at the moment, but that doesn't stop me from being happier than I have been in maybe forever.

"Holy shit," Sasha gasps out when he sees me and I freeze, looking around to see what's going on. "Hurry up and sit down and tell me who you're in love with."

I laugh as I realize why he was gasping before I did as I was told and sat at his table.

"Why do you think I'm in love?" I question with a lifted brow, trying not to smirk.

"Because I've never seen you smile like that before. And people only get that goofy look on their face when they're in love. So who is it? I assume this person has something to do with why you want me to check over your contract."

"How did you hit the nail on the head?" I question, and Sasha throws back his hair.

"It's a gift," he replies, and I chuckle.

"It's Brendon," I tell him, and his brows shoot up at a comical speed.

"Your best friend? But I thought both of you were straight?"

I nod. "So did we. Over the summer, I met a guy who

taught me a lot about sexuality, and I realized I've never been straight, but it was the only label I knew well enough to claim. When I got home, I told Brendon about it, and I guess he came to the same conclusion: maybe we had both been crushing on each other without really knowing it."

"So you're telling me I had a chance with you all along?" he asks, and I bark out a laugh.

"You know I could never handle a man like you," I tell him, and he sighs but nods.

"You're right, and Rio is my soulmate anyway so I would have only ended up breaking your heart," he replies in a dramatic fashion.

"See, everything happens for a reason. But I need you to promise you won't tell anyone until we find out if we're actually allowed to date. Neither of us can risk losing our sponsors."

Sasha mimes locking his lips and dips his chin. "Your secret is safe with me. I would never out you. Even if you just told me you weren't ready to come out, I would keep that secret until the day I die. No one should ever be forced to do something they aren't ready for. It's a personal decision and everyone chooses the path that they think is right for them. Who am I to take that choice away from them?"

I smile at my friend and thank him. "Now tell me how your summer has been."

Sasha's entire face lights up and I know I'm going to get a long ass story, but I don't care. I've missed my friend and will listen to whatever he has to tell me.

The waitress comes to get our order before Sasha starts, and thankfully I've been here a hundred times before, so I don't need time to look at the menu.

"This summer was the absolute best of my life," Sasha tells me with a dreamy voice once the waitress walks away. "It was beyond busy and normally would have stressed me the fuck out, but I had Rio by my side, and it made everything better. We moved into that cute little house that I told you about, and both worked our asses off so that we could afford the rent and put a little away in savings. Rio's parents offered to help but we wanted to do this on our own. Eventually, we'll both be making a lot more money, so it really is just for a couple of months that we need to give it our all."

I nod. "You guys really lucked out on that place. Not many people are offering rent to own agreements these days."

"Tell me about it," Sasha responds with big eyes. "It was like the universe was really looking out for us. Now just keep your fingers crossed that I pass the bar exam."

"When do you get your results?" I check even though I know he's told me before. I just can't seem to remember.

"Hopefully, any fucking day, but it differs a little every year. Once the results are in, I'll be able to move up from law clerk to actual lawyer. It's all a long-drawn-out process, but I'm beyond excited," he says with the biggest grin.

"I can tell," I reply with my own smile. "And how is Rio enjoying being a teacher?"

Sasha's face lights up even more and I love that he's that excited for his boyfriend. "He's loving it. Obviously, he's only had students for a week, but it's everything he could have wished for. We honestly weren't expecting him to get the first job he applied for, but they said that his resume was beyond impressive, and now he's a gym teacher at a high school that is only two blocks from our house."

"I'm so happy for you guys," I tell him with a soft smile. "You both deserve to be this happy, but especially you."

Sasha presses his lips together and his eyes turn a little glassy, but he blinks quickly to stop any tears from breaking free. To say his life has been crazy would be a complete understatement. But thankfully he didn't let his history break him or his bubbling personality. He really does deserve all the happiness in the world and I'm really glad he's finally getting it. He's one of the best people I've ever met.

"Okay stop being sappy," Sasha murmurs, waving me off. "You know I don't like to cry in public."

I chuckle. "Sorry. Now tell me more about the law firm you've been working for."

He sits up a little straighter before telling me *everything*.

The rest of our dinner is filled with easy conversation and amazing food, and I'm almost a little sad to say goodbye when we're finished.

"We can't go this long without hanging out again," Sasha says after we pay our bills.

"My thoughts exactly."

"I'll spend tonight and tomorrow going over your contracts and will hopefully have an answer for you by Monday morning about what is and isn't allowed," he assures me before wrapping his arms around me for a big hug. "And if something happens to be in the contracts that prevent you from coming out, know that you two can come over and hang out at my place whenever you want. Your secret will be safe with us, I promise."

"I appreciate that," I whisper, squeezing him back.

We say our goodbyes before going our separate ways, and I feel nervous but excited as I make my way to my apartment.

I still can't believe that Brendon has feelings for me and wants to move on from being just friends to something more.

When I get home, I'm greeted by Brendon and Artie, who are sitting on the couch playing video games.

"How was Sasha?" Brendon asks, while keeping his focus on the television.

"Same as usual, but even happier," I supply before dropping into the recliner chair to watch the game they are playing.

"I'm going to miss him as a mascot," Artie says before smashing a button on the controller. "Fuck that should have been a hit."

"Why are you going to miss him?" I ask with a tilt of my

head. "He didn't even get to come to any of our games because the soccer team got all superstitious and stole him away from all the other sports."

"Exactly! I'm going to miss not ever getting him at our games. Maybe we would have brought home the championship last year if we had him," Artie grumbles.

Sasha was only a mascot for one year but earned himself a mighty fine reputation. I kind of feel bad for the other members of the mascot team because they have some large shoes to fill.

"Although Izzy was saying there is a new guy on the mascot team who might be able to give Sasha a run for his money," Artie informs us. "They just better not let one team monopolize all his time this year. I mean, unless it's our team, of course."

I chuckle and nod. "We need some good luck this year, especially with you most likely being out for the beginning of the season."

Our season doesn't start until November, but Artie is looking at another six to seven weeks in a cast, plus therapy afterward to get his strength back. The chances of him being back to peak ability by November is not probable. Thankfully though, the beginning of the season isn't as important as the end.

Last year, we lost two amazing players near the end of the season due to injuries. Even though our entire team is solid the loss fucked with our heads, and we ended up getting knocked out of the tournament fairly early on.

All of us are craving that championship win this year and are willing to do anything to make it happen.

"No one is allowed to do anything that will cost us the win this year," Brendon says as the game finishes. He looks at me with an almost sad expression, silently saying, *even us.*

I nod telling him I understand without using my words.

We both want to leave GSU at the top of our game, and

even though we both want to be with each other, basketball has to come first. We've worked too hard to let anything take us down. We're also young and have our entire lives to be together. The same can't be said for basketball.

Artie's phone chimes on the table, and a goofy grin takes over his face, letting us know Izzy has sent him a message.

"As much as I love kicking your ass at video games, Izzy just accepted my invitation for a date tonight, and spending time with her is much more fun," he says before sticking his tongue out at Brendon.

Brendon flips him the bird before mumbling, "asshat," under his breath.

"Are you really going to let a girl come between our friendship?" I tease Artie who doesn't even miss a beat before nodding.

"Damn fucking right I am," he tells me, and I can't help but laugh. "Don't even try to lie and say you wouldn't do the same thing."

I shrug. "I dunno, I actually value our friendship," I reply nonchalantly. "But I also don't blame you for wanting to spend time with the person you're crazy about."

I cast a quick glance at Brendon who's smiling at me like he knows I'm talking about him.

"Did you need a ride?" Brendon asks, but Artie shakes his head.

"I'm good. She actually volunteered to drive us. I can't wait until this cast comes off, so I don't feel so useless," he grumbles.

"It's the cast's fault?" Brendon jokes, and Artie whirls a stuffed basketball at him, making us all laugh.

"Why am I friends with you?" Artie murmurs.

"Because he was kind of a package deal with me. I know I'm the real reason you stick around," I tease.

"Why is everyone ganging up against me?" Brendon complains with an adorable pout.

Artie's phone chimes again and he grabs his crutches before slowly standing up. "My ride's here, losers. I'll see you all tomorrow," he tells us as he hobbles to the front door.

"Make sure you don't show her your true colors just yet or she'll break up with you before the date's even over," Brendon calls out.

Artie shakes his head but doesn't waste his energy responding. Brendon has always been the most clever of the three of us, and it's pretty hard to beat him at his own game. That's why we usually resort to teaming up against him when we can.

Brendon might have a smart mouth, but it's always in good humor and he would actually feel bad if he truly hurt our feelings. He's only crossed the line a time or two and it gutted him. He likes to crack jokes, but he doesn't actually want to hurt us, which I really appreciate. He wouldn't be my best friend if he was actually an asshole.

"Ready to watch a movie in my room?" Brendon asks once Artie is gone.

My heart beats a little faster at the idea of cuddling in Brendon's bed. We've obviously watched a million movies together in the past, but tonight is different because things between us are different.

"What movie do you have in mind?" I check, not moving just yet.

"Whatever you want," he replies with a sexy grin. "I'll be honest. I probably won't be paying the movie much attention."

My cock takes note of his words and his sultry tone and starts to stiffen in my pants.

"Let's just watch something we've seen a bunch of times before then," I suggest and the smile that takes over Brendon's face damn near makes it hard to breathe.

"I love the way you think," he tells me as he stands then offers me his hand.

I take it and let him pull me to my feet which results in us standing chest to chest.

The air between us is thick and filled with lust and I find it hard to form any words.

"If we are alone, can I kiss you whenever I want?" he asks while staring intently at me with a look I've never seen on his face before—at least not directed at me.

My eyes immediately zone in on his lips and I slowly nod. "That sounds fine to me," I whisper.

Brendon doesn't wait for further words before he's leaning in to kiss me. When his lips touch mine, my eyes flutter shut, and my arms wrap around him as I melt into his body. The kiss isn't a frenzy or overly heated, but it feels better than any kiss I've ever had before.

"Has a kiss ever been that good before?" he asks quietly, his lips moving against mine as he speaks.

I shake my head. "Never."

"Not even with that guy you hooked up with this summer?" he questions with insecurity in his eyes. A look that I never would have thought possible coming from such a confident guy like Brendon.

"Not even him," I tell him honestly, making sure I hold eye contact with him the entire time, so he knows how serious I am.

He nods then kisses me again, this time pulling me into him so that I'm as close as humanly possible. "I've never felt a connection like this with anyone," he confesses.

"Neither have I," I reply before taking a step back and grabbing his hand. "Now come on. I think it's time we move somewhere more comfortable."

Brendon smiles, letting me guide him to his room. We immediately climb onto his bed, and he grabs the remote for his television.

Once the remote is in hand, he pulls me into his arms

before turning on the television to scroll through the options available on the streaming service.

We settle on a tried-and-true favorite and spend at least ten minutes actively watching the movie.

"You're wearing too many clothes," Brendon murmurs into my ear while his hand trails up and down my side.

I chuckle and turn in his arms so I'm facing him. "You're wearing the exact same amount of clothing," I counter with a lifted brow.

He sticks out his bottom lip and nods. "I know, and it's killing me. I want to feel your skin on mine."

I narrow my eyes at him, but I have a playful smirk on my lips at the same time, so he knows I'm not actually annoyed. "Do you think you can keep your hands to yourself if we shed our clothing?"

Brendon doesn't miss a beat before shaking his head. "Absolutely not. But would that be a bad thing?"

I chuckle and lift a shoulder. "I guess not."

Brendon's face lights up and he shuffles off the bed. "Perfect. Now strip baby. Boxers are the only thing you're allowed to keep on."

The way he calls me baby sounds so fucking perfect that you would think he's called me it a million times. And the way it warms me up inside lets me know that I hope he uses that nickname a lot more from now on.

"You're so bossy," I tease with a big grin but also climb off the bed and begin to strip.

Once we're both in our boxers, Brendon pulls back the blankets on his bed, and we climb in quickly, wrapping each other up in our arms once more.

"I don't want to rush this," I tell him as his hands roam over my skin, eliciting goosebumps.

"Why not? Aren't you just as desperate to do everything as I am?" he questions with a tilt of his head.

I smile and nod. "I absolutely am. But I want to treasure

these moments with you. You're not a summer fling and this isn't an experiment. I want us to take our time because you mean everything to me. You always have. And we have all the time in the world, so why rush? Let's take it slow and savor every experience together."

The corners of Brendon's lips turn upward, and he nods. "When you put it that way, it sounds perfect."

"Well, duh, I'm always right," I joke. Then Brendon starts to tickle me, and I quickly have to call uncle.

"We can take it slow, but I'm still going to kiss the shit out of you right now," he tells me, and I nod, inviting him to do just that.

When his lips press to mine, a hum of contentment ripples up my throat, and I allow Brendon to take the lead.

One thing I figured out over the summer is that I like taking a more submissive role when I'm with a man. When I'm with a woman, I love being in control, but something about a man taking the reins really turns me on. I also *love* bottoming, so fingers crossed Brendon likes to top. I'd obviously top him if he wants me to, but just the idea of Brendon's massive cock sliding into me has me panting with need.

With a firm grip on his hip, I buck my hard cock into his leg causing a needy whimper to come from the sexy man in my arms.

"Fuck, baby, do you have any idea what you do to me?" he questions, thrusting his hips forward so I know that he's just as hard as I am.

Why the fuck did I request we take this slow again? I'm already regretting that decision. I meant what I said about wanting to savor every minute, but I'd also really like everything he's willing to give me right fucking now.

Not wanting to continue overthinking everything I quickly move so that I'm straddling Brendon who looks at me with wide eyes that are laced with desire and lust.

"You look so fucking hot right now," he tells me, running

his hands up and down my sides. "Your body is hard and lean and the exact opposite of a woman's, but it's turning me on more than I have ever been in my entire life."

I run my fingers over his smooth chest and nod. "I feel the exact same way about you right now."

I lower myself to capture his lips with mine again this time thrusting my hips into his. His hard cock rubbing against mine through the confines of our boxers. The feeling is fucking heaven and leaves me almost lightheaded.

"Damn, baby," Brendon gasps out and I take the opportunity to snake my tongue into his mouth.

We continue to dry hump and make out and when Brendon gives me a gentle push back, we are both panting like crazy.

"You were right when you said we should take this slow and savor each moment," he tells me once he can form a sentence again. "And if we don't pause for a minute I'm going to blow and that's not how I want our first time together to be."

"How do you want it?" I ask in a quiet, almost shaky voice.

I never felt this nervous with Henley and maybe that's because I didn't have feelings for him. Everything with him was just fun and a way of exploration. It wasn't meant to be more than that. It was like it was with a lot of girls I've been with, fun and hot, but void of any true emotions or connection.

That's obviously the exact opposite of how I feel about Brendon. This isn't just a quick fuck to get our needs met. We are best friends wanting to grow something that will hopefully last. And even if it does end there will *always* be feelings for each other. That's inevitable with how close we already are. I think that's why I'm nervous. There is so much at risk here, and I want everything we do to be amazing for the both of us.

"How about we lay facing each other and jerk each other off while we make out," Brendon suggests. "But as you suggested, we take our time. Let's see how long we can last."

I smile at him and slowly move to lay beside him, shucking my boxers at the same time. "I like the sound of that," I tell him before gripping his boxers and shoving them down as well.

Brendon helps me get rid of his last article of clothing and quickly we are both laying nose to nose completely naked. Both of our breathing is heavy as we stare into each other's eyes, and I literally feel like I'm in a dream or something. There is no way this is actually real life right now.

Without breaking eye contact, Brendon grabs my hand and lifts it to his mouth, licking the palm before letting me go and doing the same to his.

"This is going to be so good," he whispers before grabbing my cock.

I throw my head back and let out a needy moan before reaching down to take him in my hand as well. The noise he makes is similar to mine, but deeper and almost more guttural. It's a huge turn on.

Our mouths crash back together as we both slowly stroke each other, needy whimpers and groans breaking through as we find what the other likes best. It's slow and sensual and everything I could have ever wanted with a man like Brendon. We're taking our time learning how to please the other and storing that information to use next time. Because there definitely will be a next time, and a time after that.

If things go how I'm hoping, we'll have plenty of times together to explore and bring each other as much joy and pleasure as possible. Forever seems like a pretty strong word to say considering we literally just started this, but I never planned on living a life without him, so it doesn't feel wrong either. Some might think that thought should terrify me but with Brendon everything has always felt right, and this is no different.

His hand is firm on my throbbing cock as he slowly slides his fist down, pulling back my foreskin while also swirling his thumb around the crown to collect the precum there and using it to make his fist even slicker.

Brendon doesn't seem to be the leaking type, so I bring my hand up and spit in my palm to help my fist glide easier over his extremely thick cock. I know it's rude to compare sizes, but he is *much* larger than Henley is and when we do get around to actually fucking he's going to stretch me so fucking wide I might just split in two. But if Brendon's cock is what kills me I'd gladly choose that way to die.

"Your hand feels so fucking good, baby," Brendon whispers against my mouth as I find a rhythm. Discovering that he really likes it when I squeeze the base of his cock and rotate my wrist when I reach the top.

"Maybe tomorrow I'll show you how good my mouth feels," I flirt with what I'm hoping is a sexy smirk.

"Fuuuccckkk," he moans the word out, making me smile even more. I love that I'm the one who is making him sound like that. Who is turning him on and eliciting those dirty noises from him. "I can't wait to try everything with you, C. I know your mouth is going to be so fucking talented, because that's just who you are. You excel at everything you do. But you know I'm the same way, and I'm a fast learner. So if you think you'll be the only one sucking cock tomorrow, you are sorely mistaken. I can't wait to see you come undone with my lips wrapped around your perfect dick."

Who knew Brendon was the dirty talking type? I didn't, but I definitely don't hate it. In fact I want more. I want to know just how filthy he can get.

"You think you'll be that good, huh?" I check before diving in to nibble on his lower lip.

He lets out a low lust-filled chuckle and nods. "You know

it, baby. And even if I'm not good at first, I'm not a quitter and I won't stop until you're shouting and coming down my throat."

A needy whimper leaves my lips as his fist starts to pick up speed.

"Does just the thought of that have you turned on?" he checks, moving to kiss my neck. His lips are hot and wet against my neck and have shivers of lust shooting through my body. "Are you going to teach me how you like it best so that I can blow your mind whenever I feel like it?" He gently nibbles on the soft spot between my ear and my shoulder, making my back bow a little, pushing my cock into his hand even more and pulling a needy groan from my lips. "Once I've mastered that skill we can move on to more advanced moves." Both of our fists are now moving at a much more rapid pace as we near our climaxes, and I'm panting like crazy as his dirty words turn me on. "Would you like to feel my cock inside of you?" he asks before running his tongue up my neck and pulling my earlobe into his mouth. "Because I don't think anything is going to compare to being inside of you. Just thinking about it has me wanting to blow." His words become more labored as our hands move quickly and honestly, I wonder how he's talking at all because I don't think I could form words if I wanted to right now.

I twist my hand at the top of Brendon's cock, causing him to gasp and thrust into my grip. "Shit. Fuck. Damn. I'm. Close," he pants out each word.

I nod letting him know that I'm right there with him. The telltale tingle of my orgasm starts deep in my spine and shoots directly into my balls, causing my movements to become jerky as all my blood flow heads directly into my dick. All I can think about is coming and it isn't going to take much to set me off.

"Give it to me, baby. Come in my hand. Show me how

much you love this," Brendon whispers and that's all it takes for me to shout out and let go.

Hot sticky ropes of cum erupt into Brendon's hand and even though I should be focusing on getting my man off too, my head is too foggy to move for a moment. But that doesn't seem to bother Brendon because he shoves me so that I'm on my back and straddles me, jerking himself off and using my cum as lube. His bottom lip is between his teeth and his lids are low as he stares at me, moving his fist rapidly. Lust is written all over his face and when he finally comes, his head falls back, and the sexiest moan leaves his lips as he covers me with his release.

He's panting heavily when he collapses beside me, pulling me into his arms and kissing my forehead.

"I don't think I've ever come that hard before," he tells me after a couple of minutes pass and our breathing isn't so labored.

I press a kiss to his chest and nod. "Me either. I've also never had someone mark me like that."

When I tilt my head to look at Brendon his brows are furrowed, and his lips are pressed together. "Did I cross a line?" he checks, and I shake my head with a big smile.

"Not at all. It was hot as fuck. Although it was a little messy."

He chuckles and nods. "Who the fuck cares about the mess. We'll just have to shower and wash the bedding. And hell we can even do the bedding tomorrow and just move to your bed after the shower."

I laugh along with him, grinning from ear to ear. "I like the way you think. Why don't we throw the bedding in the wash after our shower and that way we'll only have to dry them in the morning," I suggest.

"You always were the smarter one," he jokes with a sexy smirk. "And think of all the sexy things we can get up to in the shower." He waggles his brows at me, and I can't help but laugh again.

"Have I unleashed a beast?" I question and he nods quickly.

"Damn right," he tells me before kissing me briefly. "Now that I've got a taste of you I don't think I'm ever going to want to stop being with you. It's like I was eating the store brand of candy my entire life and I've finally experienced the high-end stuff. It's so much better and I'm going to want it every chance I can get it."

I smile while shaking my head. "You're ridiculous. But you aren't going to find me complaining."

Brendon pulls me in for another kiss, but I don't let us get too carried away because we definitely need a shower or this cum is going to get crusted on us and become a lot harder to clean off.

"Come on, sexy. It's time to get cleaned up," I say as I try to pull out of his hold.

"Okay, just as long as I can get you dirty again soon," he counters, and I chuckle loving how perfect this feels.

We can joke and laugh and still have mind blowing orgasms. It's like the best of both worlds.

I've heard people say that you should date your best friend, I just never thought that applied to Brendon and me. But now that we're trying this, I can see why people say that. Because even though it's only been a day, I'm happier than I have been in a very long time. Hopefully that feeling doesn't fade.

CHAPTER FOURTEEN

MONDAY MORNING COMES FAR TOO QUICKLY, PUTTING me in a sour mood. It's solely because I'll have to keep my hands to myself today and I'm *not* looking forward to that. Not after being able to touch and kiss Carter whenever I wanted over the weekend. Obviously, we needed to be a little discreet when Artie was home, but thankfully that wasn't very often since he wanted to spend all his time with Izzy.

As I stare at the ceiling, trying to convince myself to get out of bed, my thoughts take me back to yesterday and one of the hottest moments of my life.

"WHAT TIME DO you think Artie will be back?" I ask Carter, letting my fingers glide up and down his arm as we cuddle in bed.

"Probably not until lunch," he guesses.

"So, we have lots of time to do what we talked about yesterday then," I say, pulling my arm out from under my man and shifting so I'm hovering over him.

With a control I wasn't sure I had, I slowly lower my hips just enough that Carter can feel my already ram hard cock against his impressive erection before lifting back up.

"Fuccckkk," he hisses out, thrusting upward, trying to chase the friction.

I click my tongue at him and shake my head. "We're not grinding against each other this time," I inform him as I slowly move down his body, leaving a trail of kisses behind.

My lips land on his rich brown peck first, and I flick my tongue out to wet his nipple, which elicits a perfect moan from my sexy man. Next, I kiss his ribs, then his belly button, before making my way to his hip. I nuzzle my nose into his groin, inhaling his musk deeply. Damn, does he ever not smell fucking good?

Carter's cock is already leaking, and I lick my lips, wanting to taste him so badly but not wanting to take him into my mouth just yet.

Sticking my tongue out, I trace his balls, loving the way he shivers under my touch. I lean in closer and suck one into my mouth, smiling around the mouthful as he lets out a loud, needy moan.

"Am I doing good?" I ask with a knowing smirk.

Carter rolls his eyes, but doesn't respond—not that I need him to—his noises speak for themselves.

Holding eye contact, I slowly trail my tongue up his hard cock, stopping at the top to lap up his precum. A low groan rips past my lips as the tangy, salty taste coats my tongue. Jesus fucking Christ, he tastes delicious. I had no idea cum could taste that good, and I'm desperate to swallow his entire load. Do all guys taste this good, or is it just Carter? I mean, I've tasted my own spunk before, but I don't remember it tasting like this.

I swirl my tongue around his tip, allowing it to tease its way under his foreskin before gently pulling back the excess skin to reveal his girthy crown. Eager to have him in my mouth at this exact moment, I part my lips and slowly take him in, humming as he fills me. His cock is heavy against my tongue, and he continues to leak, coating the back of my throat with his precum.

"Fuck, baby," Carter cries out as I start to suck, taking my time, working my way down, slowly being able to take more of him into my mouth.

Since I'm not used to having a dick in my mouth, it doesn't take long for my jaw to start to ache, but I refuse to let it stop me. I want to make Carter come undone with my mouth alone. I want to erase all thoughts of anyone he's ever been with, so when he thinks about sex and mind-blowing orgasms, all he thinks of is me.

Carter's hands find purchase in my hair, but he doesn't force me down; it's like he just needed something to hold on to. I've always had my hair on the shorter side, but I decided to change things up this summer and grow it out. Considering how good it feels to have my man pulling on it, I don't think I'll be cutting it short ever again.

Determined to make this an amazing blow job, I take a deep inhale through my nose and slowly move my way even farther down his shaft, taking as much of his giant cock as I can. When I gag, I come up for air but go back down just as quickly—again going as far as I'm able to.

"Yes. Yes. Yes!" Carter shouts, seemingly enjoying what I'm doing.

I use one of my hands to play with his balls as I continue to suck him off, going up and down at a steady pace. When I reach the top, I swirl my tongue around the tip before diving back down, humming and sucking as I go. Each time I hum, Carter shakes from the vibrations, which has my own dick aching to be touched. But I ignore it and give all my focus to the sexy man in my bed.

"I... I'm... I'm close," Carter stutters as I continue to blow him.

I want to taste him, but I also don't want to let him out of my mouth to tell him that, so instead, I look into his eyes and nod at him, silently telling him to give it to me, to fill my mouth with his delicious juice.

When I dive back down, pausing to take him as far as he will go, his entire body shakes again, and he cries out as he finally lets go. His climax fills my mouth with a force that almost gags me. But I refuse to let a drop go to waste, so I breathe through my nose and swallow every last drop.

When I'm certain I've gotten it all, I slowly release him from my mouth, pausing to kiss the crown of his cock. After the brief kiss, I *crawl up the bed to pull Carter into my arms, who has a dopey grin on his face.*

"I don't think I've ever come that hard before," Carter murmurs, and I chuckle.

"I'm glad I was able to blow your mind," I reply with a wink.

Carter wiggles out of my arms climbing on top of me with a wicked grin. "You blew something, that's for sure. But you should know by now that I'm not one to be outdone. Let me show you just how mind blowing it can be."

As soon as the words are out of his mouth, he moves down my body and immediately engulfs my dick in his warm wet mouth, showing me that he really is up for the challenge of showing me just how talented he is.

I GROAN as I come back to reality, wishing Carter was in my arms right now. But he isn't, and the only thing I have is the reality that today is going to be a long shitty day.

Carter and I are supposed to meet with Sasha after school today to review our contracts with him and determine what we are and aren't allowed to do. The waiting will kill me, but there's nothing I can do about it. It's just going to be the longest day of my life.

It's good that we are meeting with Sasha and will have a better understanding of our contracts after. I just don't want to wait to be able to hold Carter's hand or sneak a kiss here and there. I want to tell everyone that we're together, but I can't do that until after we get together with Sasha.

Honestly, we probably should already know our contracts a lot better, but I'll admit that I never fully read mine through. I know that isn't smart, but I just wanted to play. Even if I *had* read the morality clauses more thoroughly, it wouldn't have mattered to me because I wasn't interested in any teammates back then. And never would have imagined I'd be interested in one now. But everything has changed now.

"You need to get dressed," Carter tells me, leaning against my door frame.

"Can't we just skip classes today?" I whine, making Carter roll his eyes.

"Stop being melodramatic and get dressed," he says before leaving my room.

Obviously, he's right, but that doesn't make it any easier.

With a dramatic sigh, I throw the covers off and drag myself out of bed. I quickly get dressed before shuffling my feet down the hall to the kitchen, where Artie and Carter are eating breakfast and talking.

"Who shit in your cornflakes this morning?" Artie asks when he sees me.

I scowl at him but don't respond.

"He probably just didn't sleep well," Carter supplies, and I huff out a breath as an acknowledgment.

He isn't wrong about me having a shitty sleep. Since Artie was home last night, Carter insisted on us sleeping in our own rooms, and I hated every minute of it. I've only slept with Carter in my arms once, but it's something that I would like to do regularly. Of course, that won't be possible if our contracts say we can't be together. We'll only be allowed stolen moments here and there, and I don't think that will be enough for me.

I always wanted to be around Carter when we were just friends, but now, the idea of being apart from him makes my chest ache. Yes, I understand that makes me fucking pathetic, but it's the truth. I'm already wrapped around Carter's finger, and it's going to be fucking hell trying to act like I'm not crazy about him.

"You probably need a new pillow," Artie suggests. "Didn't you say you've had that thing since you were a kid?"

"It's lucky," I grumble as I prepare myself a protein shake. I really don't feel like cooking this morning.

"You could still keep it *and* get a new one," Artie tells me.

"I swear to God I've never slept better since I got my new pillow."

"I'll think about it," I grunt out before turning the blender on.

While my protein shake is blending, Artie heads to his room because Carter comes up to wrap his arms around me.

"You're cute when you're grumpy," he whispers into my ear, then kisses my cheek.

"I'm only grumpy because I have to keep my hands to myself," I tell him, while turning around.

Since we are still alone, I place my hands on his face and lean into him for a soft kiss. I desperately want to deepen it, but I know time isn't on our side, and Artie could walk out of his room at any moment.

"Can we at least tell Artie about us?" I plead once I pull back.

Carter's frown gives me the answer without words. "How about we make that decision after we meet with Sasha? For right now, I think it's best not to tell anyone."

I sigh but nod. "I guess that makes sense. It just sucks. I want you so fucking bad, and I'm only allowed a few stolen moments here and there."

Carter presses his lips back to mine for a quick peck, then puts his hand on mine and gives it a gentle squeeze. "Hopefully, it won't have to stay like that, but like you said yesterday, no one can do anything that will affect the team. What we have is special, and I'd love to tell everyone about it, but we can't tell if that means putting the team at risk."

"You're right, but that doesn't mean I don't hate it," I grumble.

"I hate it too," he tells me with sad eyes. "Hopefully, Sasha will bring us good news tonight, and we can start telling those closest to us about our new relationship."

He takes a step back, and I miss his body against mine already.

I want to grab him and pull him back into my arms, but Artie walks into the kitchen at that moment, killing my chance to get just one more hit by my man.

"You losers ready to leave?" Artie asks with his backpack over his shoulder.

"I guess so," I grumble, grabbing my protein shake and stopping in my room quickly to grab my bag.

I'm the last one to leave the apartment, which means I get to stare at Carter's ass the entire way to his car. Even though the view is amazing, it's hell at the same time because I can't playfully swat it or tell him how hot he is with Artie standing next to him.

I'm going to need all the strength the universe can give me to get through today without combusting or doing something stupid.

CHAPTER SIXTEEN

Brendon

TODAY WAS the longest day of my entire life. Every time I looked at Brendon, I felt a special kind of torture. I could see the longing and lust behind his eyes, and it ignited my own feelings for him. So many times, I wanted to reach out and grab his hand or wished he would put his arm around my shoulder while we were walking, but of course, none of that could happen.

By the time our last class got out, I was about ready to die. I need a moment alone with Brendon, and I need it *now*. Thankfully, we're about to drive across town to Sasha's place, so we'll have at least thirty minutes alone. Unfortunately, that time will be spent driving, but at least we'll be alone. I'm taking that as a win.

"Do you have any idea how hard it has been to keep my hands to myself today?" Brendon asks once we've dropped Artie off at our apartment and are finally alone.

I sigh and nod. "Tell me about it. I really hope that Sasha hasn't found anything in our contracts to be concerned about. I have no idea how I'll be able to function if we need to continue to keep what's between us a secret."

Brendon leans over and gives me a quick kiss. "Tell me about it. These lips are just too sweet not to taste whenever I want to."

I shove him off of me playfully before pointing out the

window. "As much as I love kissing you, we do have places to be, so drive."

He laughs, then takes off toward Sasha's place.

The drive is fun and playful, and I think that is what I was really missing today. It's not that everything has to be sexual between us, although that is fun. I just hated how we didn't feel like ourselves today. We were trying so hard to act like nothing has changed, but in reality, everything had changed. We didn't banter like we normally do, and the joyful energy that we normally have between us was gone. I fucking hated it.

Is that how it's going to be between us from now on if there is something in our contract that forbids us from coming out? I sincerely hope not.

By the time we get to Sasha's house, the awkwardness that I felt between Brendon and me throughout the day is gone, and things feel good again. I'm back to smiling like a fool, but that doesn't stop a knot from forming in my stomach. To say I'm beyond anxious to find out what Sasha has found in our contracts would be an understatement.

"Come on in. Dinner is on its way," Sasha says when he opens the door for us, stepping to the side to let us in.

"Please tell me you ordered pizza," Brendon says with pleading eyes.

"I did, with extra pineapple," Sasha tells him with a deadpan expression.

I know he's joking, but I have to fight back against a grimace.

Brendon doesn't realize Sasha is pulling his leg and gasps. "Who would do something horrible like that?"

Sasha shrugs and keeps his stoic expression for about ten more seconds before doubling over with laughter and I can't help but join in.

"Fuckers," Brendon murmurs once he clues in that Sasha was only teasing, and I was clearly in on it.

"We are having pizza but you two aren't the only ones who don't like fruit on them," Sasha tells him while walking farther into the house and we follow behind.

"It's just weird," Brendon mutters, and I grab his hand and give it a squeeze.

"It is weird," I echo his opinion.

"Did you find anything interesting in our contracts?" Brendon asks Sasha as we enter the living room and take a seat on the couch.

Sasha sits across from us in a rocking chair and stares at us for a moment without any real expression on his face, causing panic to rise inside of me. What the hell did he find, and why isn't he telling us anything?

Slowly, a smile spread across his face, and that instantly settled the worry I was harboring. "You have nothing to be concerned about," he assures us. "Obviously, you were correct about your contracts having morality clauses, but none of the companies that you currently have deals with have anything against you being openly queer. In fact, all of them seem to be very pro LGBTQIA2+."

Brendon grabs my hand and beams at me. "Well, that's a fucking relief."

I nod, squeezing his hand and offering him a small smile. "It's one less thing we have to worry about for sure. But I'm not going to lie, I'm still nervous about telling everyone about us," I confess.

"We can go at whatever pace is right for you," Brendon promises me. "If you need to keep this just between us for now, I'm okay with that."

I shake my head, trying to keep my anxiety at bay. "No. I don't want to keep you a dirty little secret. I want our friends and family to know, but I guess coming out to everyone just makes me a little nervous."

"I get the nerves, C. I have them too, but I trust those in

our inner circle to accept us and keep things under wraps until we're ready to come out publicly."

I trust everyone, too, but Brendon and I are very different people. He's calm, collected, and goes with the flow. Whereas I'm analytical, calculated, and anxious as fuck.

Brendon squeezes my hand once more and stares into my eyes, making the decision a no brainer. Yes, I'm still going to be a ball of nerves as we come out to everyone, but I'll have this amazing man by my side to give me the courage and strength I need.

"I think you guys should also tell your agents about this," Sasha suggests. "Just in case word gets out about you two. It's always good to be ahead of things like that. And if any other companies are offering you sponsor deals, they can make sure to do more digging into who wants to work with you to make sure they are a good fit."

"Good thing we have the same agent," Brendon says with a smirk. "Won't have to have the same conversation twice."

Sammy is a great guy who has helped Brendon and me sign some awesome partnerships with amazing companies. He's also openly gay, which has me at ease about telling him about this new relationship between Brendon and me.

"I'll text him now and set up a meeting for sometime this week," I say, grabbing my phone and sending the message.

As I'm typing out the message, I think about all the people we need to tell, and I realize we are somewhat forgetting the most important people. "When are we going to tell our parents?"

"How about this weekend?" he suggests, and I can't help but beam at him.

"That sounds perfect to me."

"You two are just so fucking cute together," Sasha coos, making us laugh.

The door opens at that moment, and Rio walks in with

Pizzas. "Are we planning on feeding a basketball team?" he asks, holding three large boxes.

"I know how much athletes eat, and I didn't want to be rude and run out of food," Sasha replies in an exasperated tone.

"There is no such thing as too much pizza," Brendon states, and I chuckle.

"I think the team's nutritionist would disagree with that statement," I retort.

Brendon rolls his eyes. "She's such a Debby Downer sometimes."

Rio laughs. "Sounds like we had the same nutritionist. Now come on, and let's eat before the food gets cold," he says with a tilt of his head.

As we follow him to the kitchen, Brendon grabs my hand, and I stare at it for a moment before looking up to meet his gaze.

"Sorry, but being unable to touch you today was killing me. You better get used to my hands all over you for the rest of the day," he tells me, making my skin heat and my heart pick up speed.

"I think I can handle that," I reply quietly, grinning like a fool the entire time.

"Did we look that crazy in love when we first started dating?" Rio asks Sasha, who leans in for a kiss.

"We still do," Sasha says against his man's lips before kissing him again.

The way Rio so casually throws out the L word catches me off guard, and I freeze in one spot.

Brendon and I aren't in love: we just started dating. I mean I guess I've always told him I love him, because I do, but to be *in* love is a whole different thing. Isn't it?

"You okay, C?" Brendon checks when I stop moving.

I give my head a shake before plastering on my best smile and giving him a nod. "Sorry, I just got lost in thought for a second there," I tell him before squeezing his hand and making my way toward the table.

He follows along, studying me like he's dying to know just what got me lost in thought. Obviously now is not the time to have that conversation though so I try to keep my focus on the meal and spending time with my friends.

Of course, that's easier said than done because all I can think about for the rest of the evening is whether I'm already in love with my best friend or not.

CHAPTER SIXTEEN

Brendon

CARTER HAS BEEN in and out of LaLa Land since just before dinner, and I've been dying to ask him what the hell has him so distracted. I just didn't want to do that in front of Sasha and Rio because Carter would have brought it up there had he felt comfortable enough.

"Are you going to tell me what's going on now?" I ask as I drive us home.

"What do you mean?" he asks, cocking his head to the side.

"Playing dumb are we?" I retort with a raised brow.

Carter breathes out a heavy sigh and shrugs. "It's stupid," he mumbles, staring out the window.

I keep one hand on the wheel, and with my other, I reach over and squeeze his thigh. "I'm sure it's not stupid," I assure him.

"My brain is kind of stuck on a statement Rio made, and I guess I'm just confused," he tells me quietly.

I try to think back to a statement Rio made that would have Carter this out of whack but completely come up blank.

"Would you mind telling me what that statement was?" I request, needing more information.

"He asked Sasha if they looked as crazy in love when they first started dating as we do," he supplies for me, but I still struggle to figure out why those words left him so confused.

Is he not as crazy about me as I am about him?

I mean, for the average couple, being in love wouldn't happen before you've even had a first date, but we aren't average. Our love didn't grow overnight, either. It's been building since the moment we met. Hell, we've even said the words *I love you* in the past. Of course, we meant it in a different way. It was a friendship love, at least that's what we thought it was, but for a long time now, it's been more than friendship. We just didn't know it.

"Why did his words confuse you?" I ask, needing to know what's going through his head.

"Because we've only been a couple for like two days, and that's wayyyy too fast to be saying things like love." He pauses, then turns to me. "Isn't it?"

I squeeze his thigh again, wishing I could look him in the eyes right now, so he understands how much I mean the words I'm about to say. "Babe, we've been best friends since we were damn near babies. Obviously, we love each other. We've even said so to each other. Why do you think it's too fast?"

"That's different. It was friendship love," he counters.

"That's how it started, yeah, but obviously, it's morphed into something new and better over time. I'm already crazy about you, C, and I think I have been for a while. I just didn't know it. The second my eyes were opened to my true sexuality, everything finally made sense, and it was easy for me to see that you've been more to me than a best friend for a good amount of time. So yeah, I love you, C, and as Rio pointed out, it's obvious to anyone who sees me looking at you."

Carter doesn't respond right away, and I almost pull over so I can look at him and make sure he's okay. Thankfully, though, he doesn't stay silent for too long.

"How do you have this way of making things sound so simple?" he asks, placing his hand on top of mine and intertwining his fingers with mine.

I shrug. "I think it's because it's us. We've always made sense together, so it really is simple to me."

He squeezes my hand and nods. "I guess you're right. And to stop you from thinking otherwise, I love you too, B. I thought it was too soon, but you made me realize love has no timeline. It happens when it happens. And I'm really fucking glad that it's happening to us."

I chuckle and flash him a quick grin. "Me too, baby. Loving you is the easiest thing I've ever done."

"Should I send an email asking for a meet up with the coaching team this week?" he asks, and I nod.

"Yes, the sooner the better. I don't want to have to spend too much longer trying to keep myself in check around you."

He laughs as he pulls out his phone and sends a quick email. "Tell me about it. I honestly think keeping our relationship a secret will do more damage to the team than coming out."

"I've been thinking the exact same thing," I reply. "I was so distracted and out of it today that I barely learned anything. And it was more than just keeping my hands to myself. I was overthinking everything, making sure that I didn't clue anyone in on how I feel about you, and it made me act like a psycho. I'm sure people could tell something wasn't right with me today."

"I'm glad I wasn't the only one going crazy today," he tells me as I'm pulling into my parking spot.

Once the car is shut off, I lean over and give him a quick kiss. "How about tomorrow we try to act more like ourselves?" I check. "We won't kiss, hold hands, say I love you, or anything like that, but I think everything else should be fine. We've always been touchy and close, and when you think about it, we're a bit flirty, so I highly doubt that we'll tip anyone off if we go back to being like that."

Carter presses his lips together and tips his head from side to side. "That actually makes a lot of sense. Okay, tomorrow, we stop acting like crazy people."

I laugh and kiss him again before getting out of the car.

"Will you sleep in my bed tonight?" I check as we make our way to our apartment.

"What about Artie?" he questions unsurely.

"Why don't we tell him? He isn't going to blab, and it's going to be torture keeping my hands off you in our own home. If we're telling the coaches sometime this week one more person knowing shouldn't be a big deal, right?"

"When did you turn into the smart one?" Carter asks with a smirk.

I bump my shoulder into his while smiling. "I've always been the smart one. I just kept it hidden."

Carter chuckles as we reach the door. When we enter the apartment, we find Artie sitting in a recliner with his leg propped up and a book in his lap.

"Hey, guys. How'd your agent meeting go?" he questions, mentioning the lie we told him and making me feel like I got punched in the gut.

"About that," Carter starts, pausing to look at me, and I nod for him to continue. "We kind of lied to you."

Artie closes his book and stares at us as we walk toward him.

"Why would you lie about that? Did you go and get your dicks pierced or something?" he questions, putting an idea into my head, and I can't help but cast a quick glance at Carter, who only rolls his eyes at me before giving me a quick shake of his head. He might mean that as *no*, but I'm taking it as *we'll talk about it later*.

"We didn't get our dicks pierced. We met up with Sasha," Carter tells Artie, who looks even more confused. "We didn't tell you because we were discussing our sponsor deal contracts with him. We wanted to find out exactly what was in our morality contracts…"

LAURA JOHN

Artie tilts his head to the side like a confused puppy clearly still not following where Carter is going with this. "Are you doing anything immoral?" he questions, and I almost laugh.

"No, but some companies aren't exactly queer friendly," Carter tells him, but he still looks lost.

"Do you have a gay friend who wants to work with the same company?" he checks, and I shake my head.

"No, but recently, we both discovered we're bi and have decided to date each other," I tell him, grabbing Carter's hand. Artie's brows fly up, and he doesn't say anything right away, but then he bursts into laughter. "You two are so full of shit," he tells us while wheezing.

"We aren't lying about this," Carter states, not letting go of my hand. "I figured out I'm bisexual this summer, and after telling Brendon about my experiences and the new things I learned about sexuality, he also realized he wasn't straight. After we came to terms with our sexuality, we also discovered we have feelings for each other and decided not to fight it."

Artie blinks at us a couple of times before shrugging. "I feel like my mind should be blown right now, but it oddly makes a lot of fucking sense for you two to be together."

I chuckle and pull Carter to the couch where we both plop down at the same time and I wrap my arm around his shoulder.

"Did you find anything in the contracts to be concerned about?" he asks.

"Thankfully, no," I reply. "We chose some great companies to work for, and they are all pro-LGBTQIA2+."

"That's awesome," Artie states with a toothy grin. "So, are you going to publicly come out or what?"

"We want to keep things on the down low until after we get drafted to the NBA," Carter tells him. "We aren't ashamed of our relationship, but you know how the world of sports can be. We are going to have a meeting with the coaches to get them on our side, and we'll tell the rest of the team once practices start. But besides our close friends, family, and those that really need to know, we aren't going to be telling anyone else."

Artie nods. "Our coaches and teammates are cool. I don't think anyone is going to have any issues with you two being together." "That's our thoughts too. We also think everyone will be cool with everyone keeping our relationship to themselves," Carter says, and Artie mimes, locking his lips.

"You won't find me telling anyone. I'm not the kind of guy who goes around outing people."

"We figured you'd be cool that's why we wanted to tell you first," I say with a smile.

"So, how long have you two been a thing?" he checks.

"Like two days," Carter replies, making Artie laugh.

"Damn, you two move fast. Izzy and I haven't even made things official yet."

"I think it's different for us since we've been friends forever," I note.

Artie nods. "Yeah, actually that does make a difference. It's not like you have to go through the getting to know you stage."

"Nope, we're pretty much just adding things to our existing relationship. I don't think much is going to change for us besides the fact that we kiss now and, you know, do other things," I waggle my brows, making Carter groan and Artie laugh.

"Wait, what's changing?" Artie jokes. "Didn't you two kiss on Valentine's Day?"

"On the cheek!" Carter shouts, his ears a deep shade of red. "And it was a dare."

"It's okay, baby. You're allowed to admit your feelings for me now," I joke, leaning in to give him a quick peck on the lips.

He gives me a gentle shove, but there is a giant smile on his lips when we part.

"You guys are too cute together," Artie states. "It kind of makes me want to throw up."

We all laugh, and I notice just how much of a weight has been lifted off my shoulders from telling Artie. From the way Carter melts into me, I can tell he is at ease as well, for which I'm beyond grateful.

Coming out is going to be a process, but this first step feels beyond perfect. I have absolutely no regrets. I know things aren't always going to be this easy, and we will face backlash and hate eventually, but I refuse to let the assholes ruin what I'm feeling right now.

A yawn slips past Carter's lips, and I chuckle lightly. "I see someone else didn't sleep well last night. Think you have any energy left to get at least an hour of studying in?"

Carter nods with sleepy eyes. "I think I can manage an hour," he replies before standing.

"If studying is code for sex, remember that you have another roommate who really doesn't want to hear you two going at it," Artie calls out as we make our way down the hall.

"I'm glad we told him," Carter says, grabbing his backpack quickly before following me to my room.

"Me too, he's a good guy."

"Speaking of telling more people," Carter says as we sit on my bed. "Sammy responded to my text and said he can meet with us on Wednesday."

"Perfect. He's going to be another easy person to tell," I reply with a big grin, but Carter doesn't look as happy. "What's wrong?"

"Sammy is a great guy and is going to be happy for us, but not the entire world is going to feel the same way," he whispers.

"We've already been over this. Fuck what others have to

say. Besides, it's not like we have to come out to the world," I remind him.

"You're not wrong, but if we aren't careful, someone could easily put us on blast. We both have decent followings, and people who follow college sports know our names. If someone who is homophobic finds out we're together, they could blow everything up."

"Yeah, but that's why we're telling Sammy, so he'll be able to get ahead of things," I point out.

"I know that, but I think what scares me the most is if we are publicly outed that it could put our careers at risk. You and I both know there aren't a lot of gay NBA players, at least not a lot that are out. What if the world finds out that we love each other, and everything we've worked for goes up in smoke."

Fear is written all over Carter's face, and I grab both of his hands, giving them a firm squeeze while I stare into his gorgeous eyes.

"It's a risk, but with you by my side, it's one I'm willing to take. Yes, my dream has always been to play for the NBA, but ultimately, I could live without it. What I can't live without is you. But obviously, your feelings matter too, C, so what do you want to do?"

"I can't live without you either," he whispers, warming my heart. "We can try to be discreet about our feelings for each other in public, but at the end of the day, it's going to be hard to hide it. If someone is a big enough dickwad that they want to out us, we'll just have to deal with it because I won't let them take you away from me."

I pull him into me and kiss him passionately, pouring all of my love into him to show him that we are worth the risk.

CHAPTER SEVENTEEN

Carter

"ARE you not even the slightest bit nervous?" I ask Brendon as we make our way to the head coach's office.

Thankfully the coaching team had availability today and we didn't have to wait to get this meeting over with. We want the coaches on our side as soon as possible.

As we get closer, I feel more anxious, but Brendon doesn't seem to be fazed at all. He's completely calm and collected right now, and I feel anything but. I'm sweating all over, and my heart is pounding ridiculously hard and fast in my chest. My skin is stupid itchy and it's taking all my strength not to claw at my arms to try to relieve its intensity.

"I mean, I'm curious to see what they are going to say, but I wouldn't say I'm overly nervous. We've played for these guys for three full years, going on four now. They know us and have always wanted the best for us. I know they are going to have our backs no matter what," he tells me in such a nonchalant way that is very typical of my best friend.

Brendon has always been the go with the flow guy never letting really anything bring him down. He's never cared about the opinions of others and never lets life stress him out. He's a very *it will be what it will be* kind of guy and I've always been envious of that.

I'm definitely a more calculated person. The unknown drives me crazy, and I care what others think about me even if I know I shouldn't. I'm easily stressed out, but Brendon has always helped balance me. He knows about my anxiety and does whatever he can to bring me back to a state of calm.

Brendon puts his hand on my shoulder, stopping me from walking farther, and I turn to face him.

"I get that this meeting is causing your anxiety to flare, and I hate that you have to go through that, but I'm right here with you. You're not alone in this, and if I have it my way, you'll never be alone again. Remember when we were ten, and I told you that you were stuck with me for life?" He pauses with a lifted brow, and I nod, a tiny smile forming on my lips. "I meant it. No matter what happens, I will *always* be by your side. You are my ride or die, and nothing will ever change that. No matter what happens in that office, I'm not going anywhere."

I close my eyes, inhaling deeply through my nose and blowing it out slowly through my mouth. When I open my eyes again, I'm met with the most beautiful amber ones staring back at me.

"Are you good, or do you need another minute to breathe?"

"I'm good," I assure him. "Thanks for helping me from going into a full-blown anxiety attack."

"That's what best friends are for," he tells me with a big grin.

"Oh, are we back to just being best friends?" I tease.

Brendon's eyes take on a new lustful stare as he shakes his head, then leans in to whisper into my ear. "Best friends don't do the things I want to do to you tonight."

The anxious energy that has been coursing through my veins is quickly replaced by one of desire and I almost want to hit Brendon for turning me on moments before we are going to meet with the coaching team.

I think Brendon picks up on my mix of emotions because

he chuckles then winks at me before tilting his head. "Come on, we've got a meeting to get to."

"You drive me crazy," I grumble, which only makes my man laugh harder.

"Did you think that was going to change because we're dating now?" he asks in a hushed voice so others don't hear. "Because if you did, you were sorely mistaken. I still plan on teasing you and being the same exact self that I've always been. I meant what I said last night. Nothing is changing between us, we just get to add some really fun things to the mix."

I shake my head and can't help but laugh along with him this time. There is still an undertone of anxiety as we get closer to the office, but Brendon has done what he always does and helped me feel a lot more at ease.

I really hope he meant what he said and that no matter what happens, he'll always be by my side because I can't lose him.

"HEY GUYS," Coach Ron greets us when we get to his office. We shake his hand and the hands of the other coaches in the room before taking our seats. "What brings you two in today? Your email was a little vague."

I nod. "Sorry about that, but we thought it would be best if we had the entire conversation in person."

"If you're about to tell us you're quitting the team, we do not accept that, and we refuse to let you go," Coach Ron states firmly, bringing a smile to my face.

"We are absolutely *not* quitting," I assure him. "But we did want to bring something to your attention."

I pause, taking a deep breath, and Brendon mouths *you've*

got this, to me, giving me the strength I need. I know B would take the lead if I wanted him to, but for some reason, I felt like it was important for me to tell the coaches about our relationship. Maybe that's because of my anxiety and being able to overcome this will make telling others a lot easier for me.

"Brendon and I have started dating," I tell the coaches, who don't say anything for a moment, and their faces give away absolutely nothing as well.

"That's it?" Coach Ron checks, and I nod.

"Yes, Sir. We wanted to tell you first because we also want to tell the team when practice starts, and we were hoping you'd have our back in case we faced any backlash."

The coaches start whispering among themselves, and my head spins a little until Brendon reaches over to grab my hand, offering me some of his strength. I shoot him a small smile, grateful that he is here and that we are doing this together.

"We appreciate you bringing this to our attention," Coach Ron starts with a comforting smile. We absolutely have your back, but are you planning on going public with your relationship or keeping it under wraps for a while?"

"We want to take things slow," Brendon tells him while still holding my hand. "We don't want to keep it a secret, but we also don't feel the need to blast it everywhere. We want to tell our team and our closest friends and family, but that's it for now."

Coach Ron nods. "I get that, and like I said, we stand behind you in this. You are both two amazing men and players and having you on our team has been a blessing. However, I also feel like it's my duty to remind you what might happen when you come out. Here at GSU, we are accepting and have built a place that is safe for the LGBTQIA2+ community, but unfortunately, the rest of the world isn't always so nice. I'm sure you two are aware that the sports world can be very homophobic, and by coming out, you could be impacting your chances of being drafted. There are NBA players who are out publicly, but not a lot, and I believe all of those who are out now came out after being drafted, not before. Again, we will always support you, but I wouldn't feel right not reminding you about what could happen if the world finds out you're together."

I nod, appreciating his honesty and glad that Brendon and I already had this conversation.

"We are aware that if the public finds out about our relationship that it could negatively affect our futures, but we both agree that it's worth the risk. We are meeting with our agent tomorrow and have faith that he'll be able to come up with a plan to mitigate things if we are outed or for whenever we decide to make our relationship public."

Coach Ron smiles. "I should have known you'd be a step ahead of me."

"Having anxiety and thinking about the worst possibilities in life sometimes is a positive thing," I joke, making everyone laugh.

"Well, with that all out there, then all I can say is that you two better be at your best when we start practicing because I want that championship win this year," Coach Ron says with a glint in his eyes.

"Yes, Sir," both Brendon and I say at the same time.

We shake everyone's hands again before leaving with giant grins on our faces.

"I told you that was going to be a good meeting," Brendon says as we make our way to our car.

"Go gloat somewhere else," I tease, and Brendon grabs me by the sides, tickling me and making me laugh so hard. "Shit. Stop. Uncle!" I shout.

Brendon lets me go with a shit eating grin on his face. "That will teach you not to try and get rid of me."

I shake my head at him but can't stop from beaming at him at the same time.

Brendon is a goofball, but he's *my* goofball. A life with him by my side is something that I'm really looking forward to.

CHAPTER EIGHTEEN

Brendon

I PUT my hand on Carter's knee to stop it from bouncing as we drive to Sammy's office for our meeting.

"Sorry," Carter murmurs. "I'm not sure why I'm anxious when I know Sammy is going to be so excited for us."

"You don't need to apologize for your anxiety," I assure him. "You can't control how your body reacts to situations. I just wanted to remind you that I'm here, and if you need anything, all you have to do is ask."

"You're killing it at this boyfriend thing," he says teasingly.

"It's because I excel at everything I do," I joke back, making him chuckle.

"Thankfully, I'm less anxious today than I was yesterday. I think each new person we tell will be easier for me," he states, and I nod.

"You've always struggled the most with new things. As we tell more people, it won't be new anymore, and your brain should hopefully realize it isn't something you need to worry about."

"I love that you know me so well," Carter responds quietly.

"Perks of dating your best friend," I reply with a smirk.

Once we pull into a parking spot at Sammy's office building, I squeeze Carter's knee one more time. "Come on, handsome, let's go tell another person we're head over heels for each other."

Carter chuckles and shakes his head. "You need to work on your lines, babe."

I shrug. "It's got you smiling, and that's all I care about."

He rolls his eyes, with that perfect grin still firmly in place, before getting out, and I follow right behind him.

"My favorite basketball players," Sammy greets us in the lobby with open arms.

Carter and I take turns hugging him, then follow him to his office.

"What brings you guys in today?" he asks once we're seated.

"We wanted to give you the heads up that we're dating," I tell him, causing his brows to shoot up before the biggest grin I've ever seen takes over his face.

"Well, shit. I always thought you two were closer than the average friends, but I wholeheartedly never thought you would actually cross over into the dating world."

"Neither did we," Carter responds. "We both thought we were straight."

I nod. "But once we learned the fluidity of sexuality and started to break apart what we thought we knew, we discovered that our feelings for each other weren't completely platonic."

Carter grabs my hand and gives it a squeeze. "I was terrified at first because I thought the feelings were one sided. Since I've always been shit at keeping secrets from Brendon, I blurted out how I felt. To say I was surprised when he told me he felt the same way would be a complete understatement."

"What do you want me to do?" Sammy asks, resting his elbows on his desk and his chin on his hands. "Are you wanting to go public with your relationship?"

"We don't want to come out publicly just yet, but we also

don't want to keep our relationship a secret. We want to tell our friends, and family, and be ourselves, but we know that by doing that, there is a strong possibility someone outside of our circle will find out and possibly out us," I reply, and Carter nods along.

"We just want you to create a plan in case that happens. A way to combat the negativity and put a positive spin on things," Carter adds. "Also, we want to make sure that if there are any new companies that want to work with us, they are pro LGBQTIA2+. We already had a lawyer friend make sure that our current sponsors didn't have anything anti-queer hidden in their morality clauses."

"I can totally do that. I understand why you would be apprehensive to come out at this time. While I normally recommend getting ahead of situations instead of playing defense, I get that your situation is different. I hate saying this, but coming out now could put your future careers in jeopardy. I've seen it with other clients. And there won't be any problem with any contracts you sign having anything against the queer community in their morality clauses. That's something I always look for. I don't know if you realized it, but you two were my only straight clients," he informs us, making me pause and do a mental inventory of his clients.

"Shit, I didn't realize that," I say quietly. "I just knew you were fun and wanted to be one of your clients."

Carter chuckles. "Leave it to you to pick your agent based on him being fun."

I met Sammy at a hockey game last year when I went on a date with a girl whose brother was a hockey player. Sammy was there to cheer on a friend, and we just hit it off. He told me that he was an agent and that he knew GSU was changing their policies on athletes being able to make money off their name, image, and likeness. And if that was something I would be interested in to give him a call so he could represent me. I was so excited that I told Carter the second I got home and made an appointment with Sammy the next day. Of course, I told him that he also had to take Carter on as a client, and thankfully, he didn't have any objections to that.

Carter had a lot more questions than I did, and that was probably the smarter way to handle things. Signing a contract solely off of a good vibe isn't the smartest thing a guy can do, but hey, you only live once. Thankfully, not only did Sammy have a great vibe but he was able to answer all of Carter's questions to his liking. After that, he was able to land us some amazing sponsors and earn us a decent amount of money.

"It didn't matter to me that you two were straight, but I do typically attract clients of the queer community," Sammy states.

Not only does Sammy represent college students, but he also has a few professional athletes in his clientele, which is super cool if you ask me.

"That's because other athletes are stupid and don't know how amazing you are," I murmur, making Carter and Sammy laugh.

"I appreciate your high praise, and I'm glad I've met your needs so far. Would you two be okay with me bringing in a PR rep to help me create the backup plan?"

I turn to Carter since I could care less if Sammy brings someone else in. I have complete trust in him and know he would only bring in the best.

"If that's what you think is best, I'm okay with it," Carter responds, and I nod to let Sammy know I'm on the same page as my boyfriend.

"Perfect. We have an in-house PR rep who I think would be a fantastic fit for this situation," he informs us. "We can start working on a plan over the next couple of days then set up another meeting to make sure what we came up with satisfies both of you."

"Thanks, Sammy. We really appreciate you doing this for us," I tell him.

Sammy snickers while waving his hand at me. "It's literally my job. But even if it wasn't, you two are amazing guys, and I would want to help you. I really wish you didn't have to go through all of this in the first place, but I understand why you do."

"Things are moving in the right direction, so hopefully, one day, future gay athletes won't have to worry about this stuff," Carter says, and I squeeze his hand, offering him a warm smile.

"Let's keep our fingers crossed that the forward momentum continues, and those who have outdated beliefs don't try to undo the progress that has already been made," Sammy adds, and we nod in agreement.

Since nothing else needs to be discussed, we say goodbye and make our way back to our apartment.

Carter is quiet as I drive us home, staring out the window like he's lost in his head, which worries me a little.

"How do you feel now?" I ask, needing to know what's going on in his head.

"Better," he responds, looking my way with a wide, toothy grin. "Now we just have to tell our parents at dinner this weekend."

"Are you worried about it?" I ask, and he shakes his head.

"No, I was just thinking how this could possibly be the last time I ever introduce my mom to a partner."

I can't help but puff my chest out a little at his words.

"And how does that make you feel?" I check, trying to keep my eyes on the road but wanting so badly to stare at him at the same time to get a better read about him.

"Better than I ever could have thought possible," he replies in a dreamy tone. "You know that I only ever introduced my mom to one girlfriend, and it didn't ever feel right. But being with you is like breathing air. It's the most natural feeling. I also kind of hate that we didn't figure out our sexuality sooner because we could have been experiencing these moments together sooner."

I reach over and squeeze his knee. "Me too, babe, but we can't think about it like that. Everything happens for a reason, and maybe we had to build the friendship we have now to guarantee a stronger relationship."

Carter places his hand on mine and nods. "I like that way of thinking."

I love how things are going with Carter right now. Nothing has ever felt this right.

CHAPTER NINETEEN

NERVES OVERTOOK MY BODY, making me want to throw up when Brendon and I went to tell the coaching team about our relationship. A less severe but still anxious feeling crept up on me when we told Sammy about it. Tonight, we are going to tell my mom and Brendon's parents about us, and I feel calmer than I think I've ever felt.

I was completely expecting to be bogged down with anxiety, yet there's none to be found. All I feel is excitement and joy. I know our parents are going to be so happy for us, and I can't wait to see their faces when they hear the news.

"Damn, you look good," Brendon states with a sexy smirk as he struts into my room.

His hair is styled in a purposefully messy kind of way—all tousled and dead sexy. He's been wearing it this way since letting it grow out this summer—and I am so very on board with the new look. It makes me want to lace my fingers into it and pull him closer. I mentally shake myself and push my lust down to take in the rest of him.

A pair of dark-wash jeans ride low on his hips and cling to his body like a second skin. His shirt, a simple polo with a few subtle horizontal stripes, is anything but basic on him. It fits snugly, showcasing his lithe but athletically toned body perfectly. My mouth waters while taking him in, my tamped down lust roaring back up within me.

His clothes aren't purposefully provocative, and honestly, to the average person, he'd just be dressed nicely. However, seeing him like this, instead of in his usual sweats, is really turning me on—not that seeing him in sweats doesn't also turn me on. If I'm being honest, Brendon just has to be in my vicinity to set me on fire. It really doesn't matter what he's wearing.

"You're one to be talking," I reply, moving toward him and putting my hands on his hips. "You look good enough to eat."

Gently, I press my lips to his and smile when he pulls me into him, deepening the kiss. I allow him to take the lead, melting into him momentarily before I reluctantly force myself to pull back. I almost laugh when I see Brendon pouting, and his grip on me tightens as he tries to pull me back.

"As much as I'd love to continue and turn this make out session into more, if we don't stop now, we won't be stopping at all," I remind him, and he huffs out a breath, not looking fully convinced that we should stop. "If we were meeting with anyone else, I'd say fuck it and let you take me to bed, but we can't stand our parents up."

His grip on me finally loosens, and he sighs. "Fine, but I'm having my way with you when we get home." The words are said with a growl, causing my pants to suddenly become too tight.

"You mean like you do every night?" I check in a breathy voice.

Ever since we started our relationship, we've struggled to keep our hands to ourselves in private. We've been exploring our likes and dislikes together and bringing each other to orgasm every night. The only thing we haven't tried yet is anal because both of us want that to be special. So, we are waiting for a night that we can take our time. And preferably a night when Artie isn't home, so we don't have to worry about trying to stay quiet.

One of our favorite ways to get off is to sixty-nine since it keeps both our mouths full and prevents us from shouting when we come.

"Stop staring at me like you want to eat me. You already told me we have to go," Brendon grumbles as he grabs my hand and starts to pull me out of my room.

I laugh as he guides us to the front door, and we say goodbye to Artie.

"Izzy is picking me up for another sleepover, so you two will have the place to yourselves tonight," he informs us as we grab our jackets.

"You're the best friend ever," Brendon tells him with the world's biggest grin.

"I know I'm amazing, but it's nice to hear from time to time," Artie replies with a shit eating grin of his own.

"Have a good night with Izzy," I tell Artie before we leave.

"Do you think we can finally take the next step tonight?" Brendon asks as we make our way to his car.

My body heats as my brain takes me down a dirty trail.

"I think we can definitely talk about it when we get back. But for now, I can't be thinking about it because it would be very improper to show up to dinner with our parents sporting a boner," I inform him, making him chuckle.

"Good point. But I'm pretty sure the thought of my cock in your ass is going to be popping up throughout the night whether I want it to or not."

I groan as my pants once again become too tight.

This is going to be the longest dinner of my entire life. I just know it.

THE DRIVE TO BRENDON'S PARENTS' house isn't

long, and even though we invited them out for dinner, Brendon's mom insisted on cooking instead of going out.

We arrive at the house at the same time as my mom and she rushes over to us.

"Oh, I love your hair," Mom says as she pulls Brendon in for a hug.

"Thanks. I decided to grow it out for the summer, but I'm thinking about keeping it," he explains to her.

"You really should. It suits you," she tells him, then pulls me into her arms.

"I see how it is," I murmur as we hug. "Brendon is your favorite."

She laughs, then gently slaps my chest as she takes a step back. "I could never love anyone more than you, but I also saw you a couple of weeks ago. I haven't seen Brendon since before summer."

I already know this, but I just love giving my mom a hard time. "Mmmhmm, sure."

She rolls her eyes at me, and I can't help but smile.

"Come on, no point in standing outside," Brendon says with a tilt of his head.

Brendon and Mom talk about their summers as we make our way up the steps.

"About time you finally come over for dinner," Brendon's mom, Denise, says when we walk through the front door.

Brendon sighs, but pulls his mom in for a hug nonetheless. "It's been less than two weeks, Mom, and I've texted you every day. Do I need to start visiting every day, too?"

"Once a week would suffice," she says with a wave of her hand before pulling me into her arms. "Thank you for planning this dinner," she says into my ear in a mock whisper that is definitely loud enough for everyone to hear. "My baby boy would probably never visit if it wasn't for you."

"Stop giving the boys a hard time and let them in," Brendon's dad, Lenny, says as he walks down the hall to greet us.

Denise sighs but let's us in all the same. "Dinner is almost ready, but we can visit in the living room in the meantime."

My hand twitches, wanting to grab Brendon's as we follow his parents and my mom to the living room.

Once we're seated, my mom asks, "What made the two of you want to have dinner with your parents, anyway?"

"We actually have something we want to tell you," Brendon announces.

I'm expecting a sudden onset of nerves to take over me, but all I experience is the same sense of calm I've felt all day long.

No one says a word, instead waiting for us to spit it out.

"We're dating," I tell them, grabbing Brendon's hand.

"Well, shit," Lenny grumbles as he moves, grabbing his wallet out of his back pocket.

My mom giggles as he hands her a fifty-dollar bill.

"You couldn't have waited until Christmas?" Denise asks in an exasperated tone.

"Did you seriously bet on us?" Brendon asks, putting the pieces together faster than I did.

"Why wouldn't we?" my mom responds. "I mean, it's been obvious to us that you two have been in love with each other since you were teenagers. We've just been waiting for you to pull your heads out of your asses and figure it out yourself. When Carter told me he was bisexual this summer, I figured it would only be a matter of time before you finally got together."

"We thought it would take you both a little longer, though," Lenny supplies.

I can't help but laugh while shaking my head. It honestly makes so much sense that our parents bet on us because that's just the type of people they are. I just kind of hate that they saw something long before Brendon and I did.

"How come you didn't say something?" Brendon asks.

"Maybe then we would have clued into our feelings for each other."

"It wasn't our place," Denise replies.

"How come you only ever asked me about girls then? If you thought I loved Carter, then you must have known I wasn't straight."

"When you two were growing up, it was the norm to tease little boys about girls and little girls about boys. It wasn't until you were teenagers that we realized we should have been keeping things more open, and by then, it would have been weird to ask you if you had a crush on any boys," Lenny explains.

Brendon nods. "Yeah, that makes sense. I'm just glad we figured it out now."

"We would like it, however, if you could keep our relationship between us for the time being," I add on. "The world is still filled with homophobic assholes, and if we come out publicly before we are drafted to the NBA, it could hinder our chances of getting picked."

"It sucks that you have to think about things like that, but we understand," my mom responds, and Lenny and Denise nod along.

"We plan on coming out publicly after we're drafted. We don't want to keep our relationship quiet forever, but it's also not the right time just yet."

"We'll support you no matter what," Denise says before a buzzer goes off. "Oh, the lasagna is done. Come on, let's eat and celebrate."

We all make our way to the kitchen, and I can't stop smiling at Brendon.

Tonight went better than I ever could have thought.

CHAPTER TWENTY

Brendon

DINNER with my parents and Carter's mom was amazing, but I'm really looking forward to being alone with my man.

I didn't lie to him earlier when I told him it would be damn near impossible not to think about being balls deep inside of him even though we were with our parents. I had to work at pulling my thoughts from the gutter all evening. It was seriously a form of torture, and all I can think about now is getting home as fast as humanly possible so I can make my dirty fantasies come true.

The air in my car is filled with sexual tension as I drive us home. We are well aware of what's about to happen once we get behind closed doors. It's taking all my effort not to push the pedal to the metal, but the last thing we need is to get pulled over. That would only delay what we are both craving.

I'm already rock hard, and we aren't even touching. Carter has been very diligent in keeping his hands on his lap, and I've kept mine firmly on the steering wheel. It's like we both know that if we start anything, we won't be able to stop, and as much as I'd love to pull over and fuck my man on the side of the road, it's too risky. Neither of us want our coming out story to happen because we got arrested for public indecency.

It feels like forever by the time I pull into our parking lot when it's probably only been about twenty minutes. But minutes are like hours when you're this horny.

When I put the car in park, I turn to look at Brendon, whose chestnut eyes are filled with desire. "I need you in my bed. Now," I tell him in a husky voice.

Carter licks his lips, and his pupils dilate a bit more as he nods. "Let's see if you can keep up," he tells me before bolting toward our apartment building.

I chase after him, my legs pushing me as fast as they can go, but C always has been faster, and no matter how hard I try, he stays just a hair ahead of me. When we get inside the apartment building, he moves to his left to take the stairs and I follow right behind him. The faster we can get to our place, the better. Thankfully, he slows his pace, deciding not to run the three flights up. We're both in fantastic shape, but I need to conserve a bit of my energy for what I have in mind.

Once we finally get to our apartment we are both panting from our sprinting, and I try to let us in as fast as possible which turns out to be a struggle with shaky fingers. Thankfully though I do manage to open the door eventually, dragging Carter inside and smashing my lips to his as I kick it shut.

We cling to each other as we kiss frantically like it has been years since we've last touched each other when in reality it's only been a couple of hours.

"This doesn't look like your bed," Carter teases when we come up for air.

"Couldn't wait any longer," I inform him before kissing him again.

Our hands roam over each other's bodies as we make out. Our tongues dance together, and I push Carter against the wall, thrusting my hips into him so he knows just how hard I am for him.

"I want you inside me," Carter begs when we break the second time.

"Well, I'm not fucking you in the living room, so let's go to my room," I tell him, grabbing his hand and pulling him down the hall.

"Get naked, then get on the bed," I command once we are inside, and I close the door behind me.

"I didn't think I was one to be turned on by demands," Carter tells me, licking his lips. "But fuck is that hot." He doesn't say anything more before obeying my orders, striping bare, and climbing to kneel on the bed.

"Mmm, I'm glad you like it." I practically purr out, all dark and seductive. "Do you want me to continue to boss you around tonight?" I let my sentence hang in the air, waiting for his decision.

Carter nods frantically. "I don't know why, but I feel like I need it. I need you to take me. Pleeeease Brendon!"

My heart leaps, and I can feel my pulse speed up and throb in my neck. Apparently, I need it too.

"Fuuuuck, baby, that is the sexiest thing anyone has ever said to me, and it means more than I have words for, coming from you."

I meet his eyes and am floored by what I see there. His emotions are fully on display. He's wide open to me, and I'm humbled. I can see his lust and desire clear as day, but also the more enduring and powerful ones: yearning, inner strength, vulnerability, and love—so much love that it radiates from him and lights up my insides. I know, without a doubt, that I'm showing him the same things back.

The energy between us is almost palpable. It's thick and heady. We both know, regardless of the dynamics we play with tonight, that this —this night, means so much more to both of us.

Holding his gaze, I rid myself of my clothes — slowly, teasing him as I go. Once I'm fully naked, I reach down and run my hand up the underside of my shaft which is so hard it's pointing straight up and is flat against my abs. I wedge my thumb between, encircling myself in my hand and grasping tight so I can push my cock down and away from my body. Fuck, I've never been this hard before.

I give myself a few slow strokes and watch as Carter's eyes follow my hand. He licks his lips and leaves his mouth hanging slightly open, completely unaware.

"Do you want my cock, Carter?" The words rolling out of me in that same voice that's all fire and need.

His attention snaps back to being on my face, though I can see how hard it is for him not to look down at my body again.

"Ya... yes. I want it," comes rushing out on a breath.

"Good. Now tell me where you want it. Tell me exactly what you want me to do with my hard cock." I growl. I'm so fucking turned on, not just by our game but by how Carter responds and how he looks at me.

"Fuck, I'm so damn desperate for you, baby. I want you to fuck my ass. I need to feel you inside me, filling me so full. Take me, claim me, make me yours... please!"

"Mmm, Good. I will... because you are. You... are... mine! All mine! Just like I am yours."

I move to my dresser and pull out the supplies I'd bought the other day.

When I first brought up the topic of anal sex, I wasn't sure what Carter was going to prefer, but I was open to trying anything he wanted. So when he told me he wanted to bottom, I started doing research. The last thing I would ever want to do is hurt my best friend.

Carter watches me as I drop the bottle of lube onto the bed, along with a condom. His eyes roam all over my naked body as I move. I stay standing beside the bed and allow myself to take in his perfect, toned body. His cock is as hard as mine and rests against his lower abs, precum dripping from the tip like it always does. I fucking love how much he leaks. His body shows just how turned on he is.

Reaching down with two fingers, I swipe them up his length, gathering up as much as I can.

"Open," I command, and he obeys right away.

I pop my fingers into his hot little mouth and am pleased when he immediately closes his lips around them and sucks. I feel his tongue sliding around and lapping up every drop. Yanking my fingers out, I roughly grab the back of his neck and slam my mouth against his. My tongue dives in and hunts for every last drop of him I can find.

I pull my mouth away just as fast. "Get down on your elbows and suck me." In a flash, my man has dropped down on the bed and has taken me deep into his mouth.

A low guttural groan is torn from between my lips as he bobs and sucks, taking me all the way to the back of his throat over and over.

"That feels so good, baby. Mmm. I needed a little some-thing to tide me over before I work on stretching your tight little hole open so it can take my fat cock in it." My words cause Carter to momentarily suck harder as he moans, and a visible shiver runs through his body.

The added suction and watching his response brings me far too close to the edge, and I refuse to cum until I'm pounding hard and balls deep inside my man. I step back, hearing a little pop as I pull out of his mouth.

"Get on all fours, baby," I instruct, climbing onto the bed behind him once he's in position.

I pick up the bottle of lube and pour a decent amount onto my fingers, rubbing it around to warm it up a little bit. Once my digits are thoroughly coated, I run them between Carter's cheeks, directly over his pucker.

A shaky breath escapes his pouty lips, and he wiggles a little as I circle my index finger over his entrance.

"Breathe for me, baby, and push out," I instruct as I slowly push inside him.

"God!" he cries out in a euphoric tone that brings a smile to my lips.

"How does that feel?" I check as I keep sliding into him.

"Good, but like not enough either," he tells me.

I swirl my finger inside his tight channel before starting to press in a second one.

"Yesss," he moans out, clearly loving this.

I don't think there is anything hotter than seeing Carter like this. His skin is warm with desire. His head bowed forward as he pants and moans, enjoying the way my fingers are stretching him.

I'm trying to take my time with Carter since I don't want to hurt him, but apparently he is impatient because he pushes back, forcing my fingers to slide all the way in.

My cock throbs as C lets out the neediest mewl I've ever heard. It's fucking music to my ears and will be the sound-track to our night. I can't wait to hear just how loud he gets. We don't have to worry about our roommate tonight. I want to pull a damn symphony of sound from my man.

"Fuck, baby, do you have any idea just how much your noises turn me on?" I ask him as I spread my fingers apart, stretching his tight hole.

"Ungh," is the only thing he manages to say, and I can't help but smile.

Carter is normally good with words so the fact that I've already made him speechless gives me this heady feeling. I love that I can turn his brain to mush. I want to give him so much pleasure that he forgets how to use words at all. I want him just to feel... feel sensations... feel emotions... to feel me... to feel us, as we join together.

We've barely started, but I already know how easy it's going to be to become addicted to my best friend. I mean, I already struggle to keep my hands off of him. Now that we're crossing this bridge, I know there's no going back for me.

Like I said before, Carter is mine, and I am his.

Forever.

CHAPTER TWENTY-ONE

NOTHING HAS EVER FELT as good as having Brendon's fingers inside of me. Which has me beyond desperate for his cock because I know it's going to be even better.

Brendon steadily keeps working on opening me up and adding more fingers into me.

All I can do is groan... and mewl... and pant... as I take what he is giving me.

"You're stretched out nice and wide for me now, but my cock is going to stretch you even further. Is that what you want? Do you want me to fill you full of my cock? Because I think you need it. I think you need to take me as badly as I need to fill you."

All I can do is whine out in desperation as I push back on his fingers. My words aren't coming, but we don't need them. Brendon knows me as well as I know myself. The same way I know him.

With his free hand, Brendon reaches to grab the condom then shoots me the sexiest smirk. "I want you to rock yourself on my fingers and see how far you can get them shoved deep in your hole while I get ready."

I nod quickly, beyond excited to have him getting ready to be balls deep inside me.

I do as he says, rocking back and forth, pushing myself

farther down his fingers. I quickly get lost in the feel of the delicious stretch as I work myself over my man's hand.

It's not until I feel a sharp sting fall across my ass cheek that I come back to awareness and stop.

"Damn, baby, it's sexy as fuck to watch you lose yourself like that. I want you to feel like that again, but not until I'm inside you, and you're riding my cock instead of my hand. Got it?"

I can't answer in words any more than I could before, but I show my understanding and beg by wiggling my ass and lowering my chest to the bed.

Brendon lets out a low, slow chuckle that's full of awareness and laced with a bit of pride. It's slightly dark but completely seductive. He has me exactly how he wants me, and he knows it. His confidence is alluring, and his ownership of me, at this moment, is turning me on even more.

I hear him squeeze out more lube and coat his cock with it. The sound makes me desperate. I want to feel him so damn bad. His fingers pull from my body, and I can't help but whine at their loss.

Thankfully, I barely have any time to think about feeling empty when the heavy weight of his shaft taps across my opening. I feel him slide his length up and down before he circles his tip right where I need him.

"This hole… fuck. It's damn near the best thing I've ever seen. I can't help but want to slide in and drive myself balls deep, then grab your hips hard and pound you into next Tuesday. But I can think of only one thing better, and I have to have it. Flip over for me."

I do as he asks.

"Good. Now pull your knees up to your chest and spread them wide." I quickly obey, and Brendon leans over me and claims my mouth. It's deep, but he pulls back too soon and hovers above my face.

"The only thing better than the view I had is this one. I

want to watch you as I slide into you. Especially this first time. It will only ever be the first time once, and I have to watch you take me. I have to see and memorize every little detail, so I'll never forget... not ever." Brendon pauses, swallows, and breathes deeply before adding, "This is the last first time for me, C. Do you get that? You're it for me. I'll never want anyone else as much as I want you. I know... I know I'll never love anyone else, C, because it's you... it's always been you!"

I can't help it when a tear rolls down my temple, and I reach up to grab his head. Lifting up, I crash my mouth to his before pulling him back down with me. I pour my feelings into that kiss. Showing him that he's not alone in this.

Still keeping my lips touching his, I whisper, "I love you, B, please... make me yours."

Brendon gives me one more deep kiss before sitting back up.

A shiver of desire cascades over me as he grabs his shaft and circles his tip over me again. The lubed condom is smooth and slick against my hole. I know it's the safe and smart decision, but part of me wants him inside me bare. I feel like I need him to fill me with his load and mark me. To keep part of him inside me as long as possible. I want to have him fill me so that part of him is always with me. Maybe I'll have to talk to him about this new desire later. Right now is not the time.

Soon, the circling turns to pressure. I purposefully relax my body and push out for him, making it easier to slide in.

The thick bulb of his crown stretches me wide and causes my eyes to roll into the back of my head. I try to focus on my breathing, but the euphoria rushing through my veins is almost overwhelming.

"Jesus, you're tight," he hisses out through his teeth once the head of his cock is in.

Each of us takes a deep breath before B pushes the rest of the way into my hole.

Finally, I have him where I've wanted him for so long. He's balls deep inside of me, and it feels so incredibly right. We're finally connected in a way we were always meant to be.

"Fuck, baby, you feel unbelievable around me. You're so warm and tight," he says with his eyes closed and a look of utter bliss on his face.

"I'm gonna become addicted to feeling you around me." He states once his eyes open again, giving me a little smirk. Then his look turns all sexy, dark, and predatory again —and damn does that really do it for me.

"Your sexy little ass is mine now, baby. I haven't even started fucking you yet, but I know I'm gonna want back in here any damn time you'll let me."

"Mmm" is all I can manage as an agreement right now. He feels too damn good for my words to make any sense right now, But I'm still feeling desperate. "Please B… need… more… need… hard…now!"

Brendon smirks seductively as he stares down at me. "Oh really? Is that right? What… you want my fat cock? The one that's right now spreading you wide open for me… you want me to fuck you hard with it? You want me to pound into you… to drive you into the bed until you feel like you can't take any more? To know that you can, and to keep taking you?"

His words are like fire in my veins. My ass clenches around his girth as I pant. I'm barely able to manage a stran-gled sounding "Yeeess."

It's not enough, though.

Brendon leans over me, placing one hand beside me and grabbing the headboard with the other. Looking straight down at me and meeting my gaze, he only utters one word. "Gladly!"

Before I can even think or take a breath, he pulls his hips

back and drives back into me. Automatically, my eyes close, and my head tilts back as the loudest moan I've ever made is ripped from me. The pleasure is indescribable; it's more than I could ever have imagined.

I almost can't hear him as he keeps thrusting in and out of me. "Open your eyes, Carter. Keep them on me. I want to see what I do to you, and I need you to watch me... watch me as we each break apart and are made whole and new again... together."

My eyes are now laser focused on him. All I can do is watch... and feel. There is no room for thought or words in my head.

"Good, now keep them there." That's the last thing he says before he really starts to fuck me. If I thought he was before, I was kidding myself. My man is a beast. He uses everything he has: every muscle, every joint, and bone, and part of him he uses to fuse us together.

I can see it in his eyes. He meant exactly what he said. This is it for him... I'm it... There will never be anything better than what we have... together. Although I haven't said the words yet, I can tell he knows I feel the same. This is it for us both.

I can't help how my body responds to his, each driving thrust down is met with my rocking upwards to meet him. Sweat quickly covers us both, but neither of us cares. We are simply filled with need, want, and desire. Nothing else matters at this moment, just his body and mine.

I can tell that Brendon is getting close, but just as I'm about to reach for my cock, needing the added friction to finally push me over the edge, Brendon lowers his body so my pre-cum soaked cock is gliding against his deep golden brown washboard abs.

The sensation is like nothing else and has me immediately hovering at the edge...

"B," I cry out as my balls tighten, and the tell-tale jolts of electricity shoot up my spine. "That's right, come for me baby, squeeze me hard and take me with you," he shouts out.

It's my undoing. My back arches off the bed, pushing my cock harder into Brendon as my channel tightens around his, sending him over the edge with a roar.

Sweat glistens on his russet brow and pleasure is written all over his face as he lets the high of orgasmic bliss take over his body. When the last of his orgasm dies away, he collapses onto me, completely spent. I don't mind one bit. In fact, I love it. We're still joined, and I can hold him tight to me. He doesn't move for a few heartbeats, panting like a man who just ran a marathon.

"I think we're both going to be getting in a lot of extra cardio from now on," he eventually says, making us both laugh.

Quickly kissing my lips, lifts off of me and slowly pulls out before discarding the condom in the wastebasket by his bed.

I can't help but chuckle as he pulls me into his arms. "I don't think we need to tell the coaching staff about our extra workouts. I'm sure they'd agree it was TMI!" I state, making us both laugh again.

We both grow quiet, but it doesn't last long. "That was… wow. That was the best experience of my life. I've never come that hard before."

"Same," he replies with a smirk. "When you came, your ass was choking my cock so tight I thought I was going to pass out from how amazing it felt."

"I'm glad I'm not the only one who had an out of this world orgasm," I tell him, then press a kiss to his chest.

"It felt so damn good, I'm already craving it again, and I swear… if you give me ten minutes, I'll be ready for another round," Brendon replies in a sleepy tone.

I chuckle and snuggle in closer to my man. "How about we have a nap and see how we feel after that?"

He hums his acceptance before kissing the top of my head, causing me to melt.

Brendon has always made me insanely happy, but this feeling that I have now is so much better.

It has to be love.

I was freaking out about being in love so quickly the other day, but now I don't care. I'm in love with Brendon, and nothing has ever felt more right.

CHAPTER TWENTY-TWO

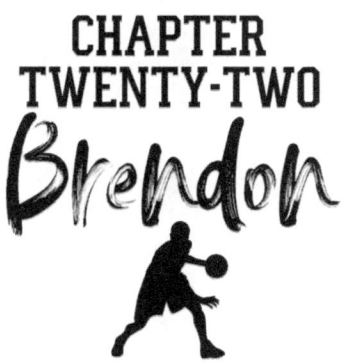

Brendon

IT'S BEEN a little over five weeks since Carter and I discovered our feelings for each other, and it's been insane in the most amazing way possible. It's like I've been riding a high that never stops. It's addicting, and I hope it never goes away.

"Yo, B and C," someone shouts down the hall as we are making our way to class Monday morning.

"Sup, Mace?" I ask with a tilt of my chin when one of our teammates catches up with us.

"Are you excited to start practice next week?" Leonard Mason, better known as Mace questions.

I nod. "More than ready. We've been getting in a bit of practice on our own for the past couple of weeks, but it's not the same as being with the whole team."

"Tell me about it," he replies with wide eyes. "Con and I have been hitting the court in our free time, but it's going to be so much better to play with everyone again."

"How is Con doing?" Carter checks.

David O'Connell is one of our teammates who was injured at the end of last season and has spent most of the summer in physical therapy, regaining his strength and conditioning his body back to peak performance.

I've stayed in contact with him throughout the summer, and since we've been back at school, but if I know anything about athletes, it's that we'll always say we're *fine* even if we aren't. So it's nice to hear from someone else that he's actually doing good.

"He's doing awesome," Mace responds with a big grin. "I've actually never seen him so driven before. He's at the top of his game. I think you guys are going to be super impressed when you see him in action."

I can't help but smile back at him. "That's awesome. Maybe we should plan a little game of two on two sometime so we can get a sneak peek at this new and improved version of Con," I suggest.

Mace's face lights up, and he nods. "That would be awesome! What are you guys up to tonight?"

I look at Carter, silently asking him if he's up for a friendly game with our friends. He shrugs, then nods as if saying, "I'm game if you are."

"We're free," I respond.

"Fuck yeah," Mace cheers. "Maybe I can get some of the other guys to join us. This is going to be so much fun."

"Perfect. I'll book a court out for us and meet you at the athletics building tonight," I tell him.

"Works for me. See you guys later," he says with a wave, then heads in the opposite direction.

"I'm glad Con is doing good," Carter says as we continue our walk to class.

"Same. I've been texting him on and off, but even if he wasn't doing well, you know he'd just say everything was good," I tell him.

"You mean like the time you broke your wrist in the seventh grade?" Carter responds with a lifted brow and a smug look on his stupidly handsome face.

I roll my eyes and shove my shoulder into his. "That was different," I grumble. "I was fine."

"The x-ray said differently," Carter reminds me, and as much as I'd love to argue, he isn't wrong.

I tried to convince everyone that nothing was wrong, but everyone saw through my bullshit. It didn't help that I literally couldn't move my hand without wincing. It was clear to everyone that I wasn't okay, but I refused to admit defeat. All I wanted to do was get back in the game.

Thankfully the break was minor, and I was only in a splint for about six weeks and back in the game two months after the injury.

"Smug isn't the best look on you," I murmur, earning a laugh from my boyfriend.

"I'd say grumpy isn't a good look on you, but you're sexy no matter what you do," he whispers with a waggle of his brows.

I fight back a groan because now I'm horny again. I thought I had a high sex drive before I got together with Carter, but now I'm insatiable.

Thankfully I'm really good at fine tuning my focus during classes and when we're working out or playing ball. But outside of those times all I think about is C and how badly I want him.

"Are you trying to give me an erection before class?" I question in my low, growly voice. The one that never fails to drive C crazy.

Carter shivers but tries to hide it and shrugs with a smirk. "Not my fault you're horny all the time."

I ball my hands into fists at my side, wanting so badly to pull him into me and smash my lips to his. "You know damn well it's *entirely* your fault that I'm like this."

A mischievous gleam passes behind his eyes, and he leans in closer to me. "If it's such a problem, we should head back to our place for lunch. But instead of actually eating, you can devour me," he whispers before stepping back and walking away from me.

I'm frozen in place for a moment, my cock hard as a fucking rock and my heart racing with pure desire.

Once I'm able to get my brain back online, I rush after Carter and grab his shoulder right outside our classroom. "I hope you enjoy being punished because you're acting like a fucking brat right now," I growl the words into his ear.

He flashes a sexy smile at me and shrugs. "Promises, promises," he responds before heading into the room.

I don't immediately follow him, needing a moment to calm myself down. Getting my head in the game to listen to our professor might actually be a challenge today. Carter has never been this flirty while at school before, and as much as it's torture, I fucking love this side of him.

Now I just have to figure out a way to make Carter feel the exact same way as I do.

CHAPTER
TWENTY-THREE

I KNOW I've been playing with fire all morning, but it's just been too much fun to get Brendon going. It's easy, too. Basically, all I have to do is wink at him or lick my lips, and his eyes fill with lust. The only time I haven't been pushing his buttons and flirting up a storm is while we are actually in class.

Once our lunch break finally comes around, I'm not surprised that Brendon practically drags me out of the school with the promise to give me what I deserve. I'm intrigued, turned on, and have a little bit of that excited nervousness that makes everything more heightened.

It doesn't take us long to get to our apartment, and the second the door is closed behind us, Brendon's lips are on mine. The kiss is rough and hard and so fucking hot. I can't help but moan as my man devours me. Taking what he wants and leaving me helpless to do anything but follow his lead.

My cock is impossibly hard in my pants, but when I make a move to unbutton them, Brendon growls, grabbing my hand and slamming it above my head against the wall.

"Don't you fucking dare do anything without my permission," he commands breathily. "You got to have your fun at school. Now it's my turn."

My breath catches in my lungs, and I nod, unable to respond but beyond turned on.

Bossy Brendon is hot as fuck. Everything inside of me is screaming to obey him.

He grabs my other hand and brings it above my head to hold them together before staring intensely into my eyes. "I know you've had fun being a tease today, but you need to be an angel now and stay exactly like this. If you move, I'll stop. Do you understand?" he checks, and I nod.

"Please, just touch me," I beg like the desperate, needy boy I am.

"It's torture wanting it so bad but being denied it at the same time, isn't it?" he questions, flipping me around, causing my palms to press against the wall.

His hands wrap around my waist and move to the button of my jeans, but they freeze there, refusing to release me just yet.

"I'm sorry," I whisper, wondering if the apology will get him to let my throbbing cock out and touch me already.

"I highly doubt that," he responds smugly.

At a snail's pace, he undoes my jeans, sliding the zipper down. His breath is heavy against my neck the entire time, leaving me a panting mess.

"I thought about edging you," he whispers as he slides my jeans and underwear down. "To give you a glimpse into the lustful hell you put me through all morning. Maybe I'll do that tonight, but I can't wait a fucking second longer to be buried balls deep inside of you. I need that needy hole to milk my cock."

Fuck. Is it possible to explode from dirty talk alone?

"Stay there, and I'll be right back," he instructs, and I nod, refusing to move.

It feels like forever he's gone, but it can't be more than a minute.

"Fuck, aren't you a sight," he notes when he gets back. "I'm really fucking glad I told Artie not to come home for lunch."

Shit. I completely forgot about our other roommate. I'm really glad Brendon didn't because this could have turned all sorts of awkward hella quick.

"How much prep do you need?" he asks, drizzling lube down my crack, causing a shiver to trail up my spine.

"Not much," I respond in a breathy voice.

"Fucking perfect," he responds, getting straight to work.

My cock leaks as Brendon's fingers spread open in my channel, getting me ready to take him. I'm desperate for him to touch me, but I know that won't be happening until he's balls deep inside me.

Slutty, needy moans slip past my lips as he fucks me with his fingers. I'm sure if anyone was walking past our door, they could hear me, but I can't bring myself to care.

"This is going to be fast and hard," Brendon tells me as he slowly pulls his fingers out.

"Just fuck me already," I plead, waiting for my man to slide his perfect cock into me.

"You don't get to make demands. You're going to take what I give you… when I choose to give it," he whispers as he pulls back my hips.

As promised, Brendon slams into me hard, causing me to cry out and my head to fall backward.

There's no barrier between us, which I fucking love. Ever since we got tested a week or so after getting together, we decided to ditch the condoms, and I don't ever want to go back. I love feeling his load drizzle out of me and knowing that I'm the only one he's ever been bare with.

Moans and grunts and the slapping sound of skin against skin fill the space around us as Brendon fucks me with everything he has. He doesn't relent until his body starts to shake, and he reaches around me to grip my dick.

"Come for me, baby," he commands through gritted teeth.

"Fuck!" I shout as I explode in his hand. My cum drips from his fist to the floor.

"Jesus. Fucking. Christ," Brendon cries out a moment later, his orgasm following directly behind mine.

His body stills behind me, and I know he's filling me with his load.

"I'm never going to get enough of you," he whispers in my ear, then kisses my neck.

We don't move for a moment, both of us enjoying the closeness.

"As much as I want to stay inside you forever, we need to get cleaned up and grab a quick bite to eat before we have to get back to class," Brendon murmurs, his lips moving against my neck.

He isn't wrong, but that doesn't stop me from hating it when he eventually pulls out.

At least we can be together again tonight. That thought should help me get through the day. Hopefully.

CHAPTER TWENTY-FOUR

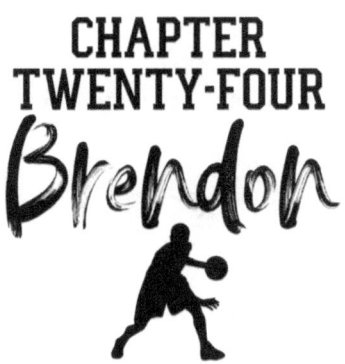

Brendon

"READY TO GO KICK our friend's asses?" I check with Carter as I park my car.

"Damn right, I am. If Con thinks we're going to take it easy on him, he's in for a rude awakening," he responds with a smirk.

"You're extra hot when you're confident," I tell him, casting a quick glance around before pressing my lips to his for a chaste kiss.

"And you are insatiable," he states when I dart my tongue out to lick his lips.

"Guilty," I reply with a smirk before stealing one more kiss. "Now come on, we've got some asses to kick."

Carter laughs and gets out of the car at the same time as me.

As we are walking into the athletics building, I see a person walking in the distance, and I wonder if they were able to see the kiss Carter and I shared. I didn't see them before, but that doesn't mean they weren't in a blind spot. I highly doubt they saw anything, but it's a possibility. If they did see us, though, there's nothing I can do about it, so I just let it go. I'm sure whoever the person is doesn't care anyway.

The walk to the court we booked out for the hour is short, and I'm pleasantly surprised to find more of our teammates than just Mace and Con.

"This is going to be so much fun," I tell Carter with a giant grin.

Carter's expression matches mine as he nods. "Let's kick some ass."

BY THE TIME the friendly game of four on four is over, we are all dripping sweat and completely worn out. None of us went easy on the others, and giving it my all felt amazing. It also felt really fucking good to win.

"I think I'm going to pass out the second we get home," Carter murmurs as we make our way to my car.

"You don't have any energy left?" I ask, waggling my brows at him.

He nibbles on his lower lip before responding. "I might have a *tiny* bit of energy," he whispers in a husky voice.

I chuckle then wink at him. "I can work with that."

"What the fuck?" Carter asks when we get to my car and see that the passenger side mirror is broken.

"Shit," I grumble, making my way to check out the damage.

There are no scratches on my car, just the broken mirror that's laying on the ground beside the tire.

"What do you think happened?" Carter questions, and I shake my head.

"I don't have a fucking clue. I mean, someone must have hit it, but you'd think there would also be scratches if it was a side swipe."

"They could have just accidentally parked too close and hit your mirror with theirs," Carter suggests, which is totally plausible. "Should we check with campus security?"

I sigh then shake my head. "Nah. I don't want the hassle. I'm sure whoever did it also has damage to their vehicle and will have to pay for it so at least they won't be walking away Scott free."

"Are you sure?" Carter checks.

"I'm sure," I reply. "If we go to campus security, they are going to want to do a whole investigation, and it's just going to take a shit ton of time. Besides, it won't be that expensive of a fix."

"Okay," Carter responds before getting into the passenger seat. "We can drive my car around until yours gets fixed," he tells me once I'm behind the wheel and I smile at him, reaching over to squeeze his hand.

"Thanks, baby. I love you."

"I love you, too," he replies, beaming at me.

While it sucks to have my mirror broken, I'm beyond grateful to have an amazing and caring boyfriend. There isn't anything that could bring me down for long with him by my side.

CHAPTER TWENTY-FIVE

Carter

SOMETHING about last night doesn't sit well with me. For the life of me I can't figure out why someone would break Brendon's side mirror. I mean it very well could have been an accident but that doesn't feel right.

Needing to get my mind off of everything, I texted Sasha and asked if we could meet up for a dance lesson today. Thankfully, he was free and fully on board. It's been far too long since I've let loose and danced, and I'm still trying to master a few skills that seem to be just outside of my grasp. Hopefully, with Sasha's help tonight, I can fine-tune things better.

"Hey, handsome, ready to get sweaty?" Sasha asks as we get out of our cars at the same time, waggling his brows at me and making me laugh.

I can't help but notice that even though I now know I'm bisexual, I still don't have any attraction to Sasha. Everything I feel for him is solely platonic, and his flirting does absolutely nothing for me.

"I was born ready," I reply with a wink, and Sasha fakes a swoon before pulling me in for a hug.

"I still can't believe all this time I could have had a chance with you and didn't know," he teases, trying to sound devastated, but there is a hint of laughter behind his words.

I give his shoulder a playful shrug. "You're ridiculous. Stop acting like you aren't madly and deeply in love, and tell me what we're working on today."

Sasha chuckles and sticks his tongue out at me. "You're no fun. I was really hoping you'd buy my act."

I laugh along with him. "Maybe I would have if we weren't both in happy relationships with men we adore."

Sasha nods. "Yeah, that does make sense. How are things going with Brendon?" he asks, letting us into the dance studio.

"Amazing," I respond in a dreamy tone.

"You've got it bad, don't you?"

"I do. He's my person," I tell him with a big grin.

"I'm so happy for you. Now let's get to work," he says, turning on the lights and setting up his speaker. "Be prepared to have legs like Jell-O tomorrow."

After having him as a dance teacher for almost four years, I know he isn't joking. Sasha is fun and flirty, but he can also be a bit of a drill sergeant—although I love that about him.

Sasha is so passionate about dance, and he's drilled the love into me. When I first started learning ballet, it was to make me a better basketball player. Eventually, I was no longer doing it to make myself better on the court; I was doing it because I love to dance. I love the challenge of learning new skills and working my ass off to master them. Even though Sasha and I don't meet up regularly anymore, I still try to dance on my own when I have the time. But I'll admit it is more fun with my friend by my side, pushing me to be my best.

Music fills the space, and Sasha walks me through a warmup exercise.

I allow myself to get lost in the movements and let the outside world disappear for the time being. Dance and basketball are the two things that allow me to completely center myself and forget about my worries. It's one of the only times my head is completely clear of anything except what I'm doing. My anxiety doesn't seem to exist either, which is rare for me.

Time flies by as I follow Sasha's instructions and before I know it, an hour has passed and our session is over.

I wipe the sweat from my brow and my bare chest, and Sasha does the same.

"You clearly have been practicing at home," Sasha notes before taking a guzzle of water from his bottle.

"I try to as often as I can, but it can be tricky," I reply, drinking a decent amount of my own water.

"Because you'd rather have sex?" he checks, making me spit out a mouthful of water.

I laugh along with Sasha as I wipe my mouth and flip him the bird. "I mean, can you blame me for liking sex?" I question with a raised brow.

He presses his lips together as if to think about it but then quickly shakes his head. "No. I can't blame you. Sex is pretty amazing."

I chuckle and grab my shirt off the floor. "It's even better with the person you're crazy about," I add.

Sasha nods, putting on his own shirt. "I couldn't agree more. We're two lucky guys to have found men who care about us and love us unconditionally."

I smile at him, and my heart fills with warmth. Brendon really does love me unconditionally. It's something that is undeniable. He'd do anything for me, and me for him.

Brendon holds my heart, and I know that he will never break it.

I follow Sasha out of the building to our cars that are parked side by side, but before I get behind the wheel I notice a note under my wiper.

"What's that?" Sasha checks, and I shrug before opening it.

. . .

Stay away from him!

I STARE AT THE WORDS, reading them over and over again, trying to figure out just what the fuck they mean.

"Do you have someone who is secretly in love with you and doesn't know about Rio?" I ask Sasha, showing him the note.

He frowns, shaking his head. "Not that I know about. Our relationship is pretty public, so you'd think most people would know I'm locked down."

"Do you think it's a friend of Rio's who thinks you're having an affair?" I check.

I didn't see anyone in the parking lot when we got here, but maybe they had seen us hugging and jumped to the wrong conclusion.

"I don't think so, but even if it is, we know the truth. Whoever wrote that note is an idiot and not someone you have to worry about," he assures me, and I nod.

"Yeah, you're right," I reply, crumpling up the note. "Sometimes people are just crazy."

We say our goodbyes with the promise to meet up for dinner on the weekend. Then we both leave to head to our places.

My chest feels tight as I make the drive home, and I can't help but wonder if the note maybe was referring to someone other than Sasha. Maybe the person meant Brendon. But how would they know about us? We've done a pretty good job of keeping our relationship on the down low. And even if they did find out about us, who would want to keep us apart?

My palms are sweaty by the time I pull into my parking spot.

I fucking hate having anxiety sometimes.

I know deep down that this note is not a big deal, and I just have to let this go.

Unfortunately, that's always easier said than done.

CHAPTER TWENTY-SIX

CARTER WAS beyond tired when he got home last night after his dance lesson with Sasha and was extra cuddly when we went to bed. I didn't think much of it until we woke up and he still seems off.

Carter's anxiety has been at an all-time low the past month, but this morning, he's on edge. I'm afraid he's going to try and crawl out of his skin if I don't help him work through whatever is bothering him.

"What's wrong?" I ask as we're eating breakfast.

"Sometimes I really hate that you know me so well," he murmurs around his mouthful of food.

"Deflecting isn't going to stop me," I inform him, and he sighs.

"It's nothing," he mutters, keeping his gaze on the table.

I reach over to grab his hand and give it a squeeze. "It's clearly not nothing. You've got bags under your eyes and you're jittery as hell which only happens when you're anxious. So what's got you out of sorts?"

"Someone left a stupid note on my car last night and for some reason it's throwing me off kilter," he tells me.

"What did the note say?" I check.

I know Carter said it was stupid, but it has to be more than just something silly to have him worked up like this.

"All it said was '*stay away from him*'," he informs me with a shrug. "I just don't know *who 'him'* is." He puts air quotes around the word him and I nod along, trying to come up with a response that will help ease his worries.

"Well, you were with Sasha, so they probably meant him, but doesn't everyone know he's with Rio?"

Carter hums. "Yeah that's what we thought at first, too. But for some reason I can't help thinking that someone knows about us and for whatever reason doesn't want me to be with you."

Aww, now I see the real reason for his anxiety.

"Babe, even if someone does know about us they aren't going to keep me away from you," I assure him. "You're the only person I want. It's me and you for life. Nobody else stands a chance."

He sighs, squeezing my hand that is still holding his. "Yes, I know that. I guess I've just been obsessing about people having an issue with our sexuality more than anything, and it didn't occur to me that someone could be pissed that I'm the one who's with you, instead of them. I really shouldn't be surprised though. You've always had a lineup of women wanting to be with you."

"I can't help how anyone else feels or what they want. I only care about how we feel," I respond, hating that he's feeling insecure at this moment. "All I can do is continue to show you how much I love you. I'm sorry the note bothered you, but I promise you, you are the only person for me. I don't have eyes for anyone but you."

A small smile slowly spreads across Carter's lips, and he nods. "Deep down I know that. I guess I just let my insecurities get the best of me. I trust you, Brendon, and know that you love me just as much as I love you, and I'm sorry for letting those stupid words get in my head."

"It's okay to feel like that as long as you don't keep it to yourself. Let me be there for you. Let me help you work through those feelings when they come up, because they'll probably come up again. I want to be your rock, and I don't ever want you to think I don't care about your feelings."

Carter beams at me before scooting his chair closer so he can lean in for a kiss. "I don't know what I did to earn a man like you, but I'm glad you're mine," he whispers against my lips.

"I'm yours, and you're mine," I tell him before sealing my lips to his.

We melt into each other and although the kiss starts off innocent, it quickly turns heated. My body is desperate to show him that he's the only person who can turn me on like this.

I lick the seam of his lips and smile as he lets me in. His tongue immediately meets mine allowing the two to dance together. Needy moans rumble up both our throats as I pull Carter out of his chair, making him straddle me.

"Jesus!" Artie shouts, stopping us in our tracks. "Seriously, guys! No fucking in the kitchen," he grumbles stomping toward the cupboard to grab a cup and fill it with water.

"Sorry," Carter and I murmur at the same time as we untangle from each other.

"Are you really sorry?" Artie asks lifting a brow at us to show he doesn't believe our bullshit.

"I mean, I'm sorry you saw it," I add, making Artie roll his eyes and Carter blush.

"It's going to be a long seven months, isn't it?" Artie murmurs with a smirk on his lips.

I'm taking his grin to mean that he's happy for us, even if he doesn't want to see us getting it on, which I totally don't blame him for. I'm not actually an exhibitionist; I just struggle to keep my hands off of Carter, especially when we are in our apartment.

"We'll do better at keeping things PG in shared spaces," Carter tells Artie.

"That's all I ask," Artie replies. "Now, if you two are done dry humping at the kitchen table, would one of you be able to drive me to school?"

I can't help but laugh. "What, you can't drive yourself?" I tease.

He flips me off in response and Carter and I get up from the table at the same time.

"We just have to grab our bags, and we'll be ready to go," Carter tells him as I clean up our dishes.

"Do you mind if we stop for coffee before class?" Carter asks as we're heading to the elevator, yawning at the end of his question.

"I'm sorry you didn't sleep well last night," I say, giving his shoulder a squeeze.

He waves me off and offers me a small smile, but it's clear just how exhausted he is by the dark circles under his eyes. "I'll be fine as long as I can get a large cup of deliciously caffeinated beverage."

"Sleep is healthier," I retort.

"Maybe you can wear me out later, and I'll sleep like a baby," he whispers, but clearly Artie hears it because he groans.

"You two have got it bad," he grumbles.

I shrug. "We do, and I wouldn't have it any other way."

Carter beams at me, and I can see the love in his eyes.

"I'm happy for the two of you. It honestly makes so much sense that you two fell for each other. You really are a perfect couple."

I'm glad he sees just how good Carter and I are together.

Hopefully, if there really is someone telling Carter to stay away from me, they'll quickly see that Carter and I are made for each other and will back off. I'm completely off the market, and no matter how badly someone else may want me, they won't be able to have me.

The drive to school isn't long and I park Carter's car near

where Artie's class is, which also happens to be near an awesome coffee shop. It means a longer walk for Carter and I but our first class isn't for another hour anyway, so we have lots of time.

Carter opens the door to the coffee shop for us and grimaces. "I'm not sure what I just touched, but I need to wash my hands," he grumbles, wiggling his fingers in disgust. "You know my order," he states before rushing off.

"Hey, B," someone calls out to me as I'm waiting in line.

I turn to find Matais, a classmate who was my assigned partner in one of my courses last year, coming toward me with his too big glasses and a toothy grin.

"Hey, man," I greet him. "How was your summer?"

"It was okay," he responds with a shrug. "Pretty boring, but I appreciate you responding to my texts.

I wave him off. "That's what friends do," I tell him, even though I'd consider him more of an acquaintance than a friend.

If I'm being honest, I probably wouldn't have a clue who Matais is if we didn't have that project together last year. We run in two completely different circles, but he was always so nice to me and he really carried our assignment last year. I felt like the least I could do was try and be friendly with him even after our class was over.

"Anything new going on in your life?" he checks, and my thoughts immediately drift to Carter, but I'm not close enough with Matais to let him in on the secret.

I shrug. "Not a whole hell of a lot. Summer was a blast, and now it's back to the grind."

He nods. "We should hang out sometime," he offers like he's done multiple times, but I always seem to drop the ball because my life is super busy.

Instead of lying to him and saying yes, I decide to go with the truth. "I'd love to, but life is about to get really busy," I tell him before the barista calls on me.

I give her my order and pay before turning back to Matais.

"Oh, I'm sorry," he mutters, frowning and looking at the floor.

"It's nothing against you," I assure him, hating how sad he looks. "I had a blast working on that assignment with you last year, and the memes you send me always make me laugh, but basketball kind of runs my life."

He nods. "Well, if you ever get some free time, hit me up. My number is still the same."

"Sorry, that took so long," Carter says, coming up to stand beside me. "I guess everyone had to take a piss this morning." He pauses when he realizes Matais is there and waves at him. "Sorry. I didn't mean to cut off your conversation."

"It's fine," Matais responds in a cooler tone than I'm used to from him.

"Did you put in our order?" Carter checks with me, and I nod.

"Yup. You'll have your stupidly sweet coffee before you know it."

Carter beams at me, and I really wish I could pull him into my arms right now.

Matais clears his throat, making me feel bad that I forgot about him for a moment.

"I should get going," he tells me. "But if you have any free time, text me."

I nod and wave as he walks away.

"Who was that guy?" Carter asks once Matais is out of the building.

"My assignment partner from last year," I remind him.

"Oh, right," he says, putting the pieces together.

I feel like a dick for always blowing off Matais because I know he doesn't have a lot of friends, but my life really is crazy. Working on new friendships isn't something I have the time for.

"Poor guy doesn't have many friends, does he?" Carter checks, and I shake my head.

"I wish I had the time to be his friend because he was super nice to me when we were partners, but I've already got my hands full," I tell him.

"With me, you mean?" he questions in a quiet voice, waggling his brows at me and making me laugh.

"Absolutely! You are more than a handful," I whisper, wishing I could kiss him.

Carter nibbles on his lower lip, and I know he's thinking the same thing.

Thankfully our order is ready at that moment, giving us something to distract ourselves with.

I know we are supposed to be keeping our relationship under wraps at school but that is turning out to be much more of a challenge than I initially thought it would be.

CHAPTER TWENTY-SEVEN

Carter

BRENDON and I walk into the restaurant that Sasha invited us to, hand in hand, since we aren't in a place where most people would recognize us. We are five minutes later than we were supposed to be, but that's not new for us. We are often late for things after school because we've spent the entire day with pent up sexual frustration, and we need to release it the second we get home.

"You've got sex hair," Sasha notes quietly with a shit eating grin as we take our seats across from him and Rio.

"Is that a problem?" I counter with a smirk.

Sasha used to make me blush every time we were together, but I've gotten used to his mouth and now give it back just as hard.

"I don't think I like how much I've rubbed off on you," Sasha murmurs, and the rest of us laugh. "You were more fun when you would turn red and forget how to talk."

"I can still make him blush," Brendon gloats to Sasha, sticking his chest out to show just how proud of himself he is.

"I could probably still make him blush if I wanted to," Sasha retorts. "I just respect our relationships."

"Aww, are you jealous?" Rio asks Sasha, who's pouting.

I can't help but chuckle before kicking at Sasha's leg under the table. "Stop being a baby. You know I still love you like a brother."

That seems to bring a smile back to his face. "That's true, and maybe now that Brendon has been promoted from best friend to boyfriend, I can claim the open spot."

I laugh and shrug. "Do you think you've earned the title of best friend?"

Sasha places his hand on his chest and fakes a gasp. "I'm offended you even have to ask that. Have I not been the best dance instructor you've ever had?"

"You are the *only* dance instructor I've ever had," I remind him, and he waves me off.

"Tomayto, tomahto," he replies. "And I know you're going to say that Artie has known you longer, but we all know I'm more amazing."

I chuckle while shaking my head at him. "If the title means so much to you, you can have it."

Sasha cheers, making people look at us, and Rio pinches the bridge of his nose. "You are too much sometimes," he mutters under his breath.

"Yeah, but you still love me," Sasha retorts.

"Yeah, I do," Rio replies, leaning in for a brief kiss.

"Have you got any new notes?" Sasha asks once they pull apart.

I shake my head, thankful that the rest of the week has been quiet. I know it's only been three days, but I'm praying that the person has moved on and won't bother me again. For all I know, it was a misunderstanding, and the person has figured that out by now.

"Well, that's good. I'll admit I was a little creeped out for you," Sasha states.

"Me too," I murmur. "It caused my anxiety to spike, but Brendon has been pretty good about helping me work through it."

"I bet he has been," Sasha replies, winking at me.

"I hate that I haven't hung out with you more," Brendon tells Sasha. "You're lots of fun."

Sasha throws his hair back. "I know. I'm the best."

"And you're not conceded at all," Rio adds with a smirk.

Sasha rolls his eyes but doesn't argue.

We fall into easy conversation after the waitress takes our order, and we spend the evening talking, laughing, and enjoying an amazing meal. I'm honestly shocked when I check my phone and realize two hours have passed.

"Time sure flies when you're having fun," I state, and everyone nods.

"We have to make this a regular thing," Sasha says as the waitress brings us our bills, and we pay.

"We really do," Brendon agrees. "But our schedules are going to start getting really busy."

Sasha shrugs. "I get that, but we can still make things work, I'm sure."

I nod. "We'll figure something out."

We walk out to our vehicles at the same time, but I stop in my tracks when my eyes land on my car.

Sasha gasps. "Holy shit."

All four of my tires are slashed, and my headlights are smashed.

"Who the fuck would do that?" Brendon growls, wrapping his arms around me.

"Do you think it's the same person who left me the note?" I ask quietly.

"If it is, shit's getting out of hand. We need to file a report," Brendon tells me, and I sigh but nod.

So much for going home.

"We'll wait with you and give you a ride home once it's all done," Rio tells us.

"Thanks, but you don't have to do that," I reply.

"It's what best friends do," Sasha tells me with a soft smile. "Plus, it never hurts to have a lawyer around—or an almost lawyer," he murmurs.

I chuckle. "Well, thank you. I appreciate it."

Brendon calls the non-emergency line for the police, and Sasha grabs my hand as I stare at my fucked-up car.

"Want to see if the restaurant has outside security cameras?" he checks.

"I guess so," I murmur, allowing him to pull me back inside.

"Did you forget something?" the hostess checks.

"No. We were wondering if you possibly had security cameras outside. My car was vandalized," I explain, and she gasps.

"Oh no. I'm so sorry to hear that. Let me get the owner," she tells me before rushing away.

"Why the hell would someone do something like this?" I ask Sasha as we wait.

"Sometimes people are just crazy," he responds.

"Mary-Beth tells me you wanted to check our security footage," an older man with white hair says, and I nod.

"Yeah, my car got vandalized, and we were hoping that if you had cameras outside, they might have caught the person who did it."

"I wish we did, but our cameras only show the front door, not the parking lot," he informs us, killing the small amount of hope I had left.

"Well, thank you anyway," I respond.

"I'm sorry. Did you call the police?" he checks.

"Yeah, my boyfriend was on the phone with them when we came in."

"Hopefully, they can catch the person who did this," he replies.

I nod before heading back outside with Sasha by my side.

"The cops will be here soon," Brendon grumbles when he sees us, flexing his hands by his side and clenching his jaw.

I don't think I've ever seen him this mad before. At least not in a very long time. Brendon is such a happy go lucky guy that it takes a lot to get him like this.

"You need to calm down," I state, moving toward him and pulling him into my arms as soon as I'm close enough.

"I just hate that someone did this," he murmurs, squeezing me tightly and kissing my hair.

"I know," I tell him, pulling back a little to stare into his eyes. "I'm not happy about it either, but we can't let whoever did this have power over us. Whoever did this wants to upset us. We can't give them that satisfaction."

Brendon inhales deeply through his nose before slowly blowing it out, never once looking away from me. Finally, a slow smile spreads across his lips, and he gives me a brief kiss.

"This is why we are perfect for each other," he whispers before pulling me back into his arms.

I might be a bit stressed out that someone is targeting me, and we don't entirely know why. But I also know that Brendon and I are completely solid, and we'll be able to get through anything.

CHAPTER TWENTY-EIGHT

Brendon

CARTER HAD to run to his mom's house Sunday morning to help her with a couple of things, and as much as I wanted to help, I knew it was good for the two of them to have some time alone.

It also didn't hurt that Carter promised me a surprise at some point today.

Thankfully, my car was booked to go into the shop yesterday, and we were able to pick it up the same day. Carter's is booked to go in on Monday, but it's not like we usually need two vehicles.

I'm busy studying when the buzzer for our apartment goes off on my phone.

My brows pull together because I wasn't expecting anyone, and Artie is out with Izzy again.

With a shrug, I swipe open the app and ask who's there.

"Delivery for Brendon Jackson," a man tells me, and I hit the button to let him up.

Excited energy rushes through my veins as I wait for the man to bring up whatever he is delivering. I didn't order anything, but I think this must be the surprise Carter was talking about. I mean, what else could it be?

It doesn't take long for a knock to come on our door, and I rush over to open it. A guy who looks to be about twenty is holding a giant basket of goodies, and I smile at him as he hands me a tablet to sign, confirming that I have accepted the order.

After that is done, he hands me the basket and gives me a little wave. "Have a good one," he says before walking away.

I'm practically vibrating with excitement as I take the basket to my bedroom.

My brain is going a mile a minute trying to come up with ideas as to what's in the basket. Knowing Carter can be a tease and a brat, I wouldn't put it past him to fill this basket with sex stuff.

I get myself situated on the bed and begin to unwrap the basket, smiling from ear to ear as I pull out each item.

Unfortunately, the basket isn't filled with sex things, but it is filled with all of my favorites. I pull out a Hershey's Symphony milk chocolate with almonds and a giant toffee candy bar first, and my mouth waters, and I want to eat it already. But there are a fuck ton more items inside, so I don't stop to eat the delicious chocolate just yet.

Next, I pull out a bag of animal crackers and snicker because I only allow myself to eat them once in a blue moon. I know they are childish, but they are a comfort snack for me.

I think the last time I ate these was when I was struggling to get my assignment done with Matais last year.

My smile stays permanently in place as I pull out goodie after goodie. There's Sunkist grape soda, a Whatchamacallit bar, a box of Better Cheddars, a bag of Fritos Twists Corn Snacks—in honey BBQ flavor, of course—and a shit ton of my favorite guilty pleasure items.

Along with all the junk food is a stuffed basketball to add to our ever-growing collection and a packet of basketball trading cards.

Clearly, Carter put a lot of thought and effort into this basket, and it really warms my heart. I just wonder when he had the time to put this all together. It's not like we spend a lot of time away from each other these days.

I pull out my phone to send him a text, thanking him for the awesome gift.

It doesn't take him long to respond, but it's not the message I was expecting.

Carter: I didn't send you a gift basket.

I STARE at my phone for a minute, thinking he must be joking. Who else would send me a gift like this?

All of the items are very specific to me, so whoever sent this knows me very well.

Wondering if maybe I missed a note I quickly start to dig through the items on my bed. Eventually I find a little envelope with my name on it and quickly snatch it up, tearing it open as fast as possible.

You deserve a man who will treat you as special as you are.

I can be that man for you.

~M

WHO THE HELL IS M?

The handwriting looks familiar to me, but I can't put my finger on why at this moment. I scratch my head before taking a screenshot of the note and send it to Carter.

My phone starts to ring a moment later and I quickly answer Carter's call.

"That's the same handwriting as the note that was on my car," he tells me once I pick up.

A pit forms deep in my stomach from his words, and a chill rushes down my spine.

"The cops have that note, right?" I check.

"Yeah. Thankfully, when I crumbled it up, I threw it in my car and was able to give it to them on Friday."

"Do you think I should tell the detective about this?" I ask him.

"Call Sasha first," he suggests, sounding just as freaked out as I feel.

"Okay, I'll do that, then I'll call you back," I inform him.

"Don't worry about that. I'm done helping my mom and will be home soon."

Instant relief floods through my body knowing that my man will be by my side soon.

"Okay. See you soon," I tell him before ending the call and dialing Sasha.

"Hello?" Sasha answers, sounding confused. I don't blame him since I don't think I've ever called him before.

"Hey Sasha, it's Brendon. Carter told me to call you."

"Is he okay?" he asks in a panicky tone.

"He's fine, but I got a gift basket today. I thought it was from Carter because the items inside were all my favorite things but when I thanked him he told me he didn't send it. I found a note and the handwriting is the same as the one that was left on Carter's car," I explain.

"What did the note say?" he asks, and I forward the picture of the note to him. "Well, shit. Clearly, someone is obsessed with you. Do you have any idea who it could be?"

I shake my head even though he can't see me. "Not a fucking clue, and *M* could literally be anyone. All we know is it's a man. But why would a guy be obsessed with me on this kind of level? As far as anyone knew, I was straight."

"Just because you're straight doesn't mean a guy couldn't

fall for you," he points out. "You said the gifts were very specific, do you think it could be a teammate?"

"I don't think so. I mean, you'd think I would have picked up some vibes if it was, don't you?"

"Maybe," he murmurs. "But you haven't exactly seen everyone since you and Carter started seeing each other. It's possible they were able to keep their feelings for you on lock when they thought you were straight, but now that they realize you're bi they are hoping for a shot."

"We start practice tomorrow and have already told the coaches that we are going to announce our relationship to the team then," I inform him. "If it *is* someone on the team, our announcement should piss them off."

"You're not wrong. Keep a close eye on everyone and tell Carter to do the same."

"Should I bring the note to the cops?" I check, still feeling uneasy about the situation.

"Yes. I would suggest doing it as soon as possible," he tells me. "They could try and trace the basket back to the person who sent it."

"I still can't believe this is happening to us," I murmur.

Sasha sighs. "I know, and I'm sorry you're going through this. It isn't an easy situation for anyone. But if you need a listening ear, I'm always here."

I thank him, end the call, and throw myself back on the bed, staring at the ceiling.

Who the hell is M, and how do I get them to back the fuck off?

CHAPTER TWENTY-NINE

MY HEART IS RACING, and my anxiety is through the roof as we wait for all our teammates to enter the locker room.

I really can't see one of our teammates being the one who slashed my tires or told me to stay away from Brendon, but I also don't have a single clue who else it could be, either. The person who is doing this must be unhinged, and none of our friends are like that, but maybe we just don't know some of these people as well as we thought we did.

Once everyone is in the locker room, Coach Ron gets everyone's attention then tells them that Brendon and I have an announcement.

"Hey guys," Brendon starts, and I feel dizzy. "Carter and I wanted you all to know that we are dating." He pauses, grabbing my hand and shooting me a warm smile that melts most of my worries away. He winks at me before turning his attention back to the guys, and I do the same. "We wanted you guys to be some of the first to know since this team is like a family. With that being said, we want to keep our relationship mostly to ourselves and those closest to us for the time being. We would appreciate it if you respected our wishes and didn't tell anyone. We will eventually come out publicly, but we don't know when we will be doing that."

I watch all the guys in the locker room closely, trying to

see if anyone seems angry by what Brendon just said. There are lots of shocked faces—which we were expecting—but none appear pissed off like you'd think they would if they were secretly in love with Brendon.

"I didn't know you guys were gay," Mace states with a tilt of his head like he's studying us.

His expression is one of curiosity, not animosity, but the question alone has me wondering if he's possibly the M from the note.

"We're bi, but we didn't really know either until recently," I inform him, keeping my eyes trained on him, looking for any signs that he might be the guy we're looking for.

He pursues his lips, nodding for a moment before shrugging. "I'm happy for you guys, and your secret is safe with me," he says with a big grin, appearing genuine in his response.

Well, that rules him out as a suspect, at least for now.

Our other teammates join in on voicing their acceptance of our relationship and promise to keep our secret. Not one of them seems upset, which causes a mixture of relief and annoyance to rush through my body. I'm happy that our friends are on our side, but I'm also annoyed that we are at another dead end for figuring out who is obsessed with Brendon.

The cops told us that they'll try and figure out who sent the gift basket to Brendon but not all delivery companies keep the best records. I'm trying to keep my hopes up that the company this guy used isn't one of those, but it's hard when everywhere we turn we keep hitting one wall after another. It's beyond frustrating.

"Just a reminder that homophobia of any type will not be tolerated at all," Coach Ron tells everyone in a booming voice. Everyone nods their heads in agreement, and Coach smiles. "Okay, with that announcement out of the way, it's time to get our heads in the game," Coach Ron says, clapping me on the shoulder and tilting his head, silently telling us to take a seat.

Brendon and I nod at him before heading over to a bench with open space, our hands still firmly grasped together.

We might not have found out who's obsessed with Brendon, but at least we have the support of our team and don't have to hide our love from them.

Since today is our first practice of the season, Coach's speech isn't a long one because he mainly wants to get us on the court and there isn't much to discuss yet. That will change after our first game and throughout the rest of the season.

A small amount of anxious energy still courses through my veins as we make our way to the court, but it quickly fades away once I get a ball in my hand and start warming up. There's a chance it will come back after we are done with practice, but at least for the time being, my head is clear.

THE WHOLE TEAM is dripping sweat by the time practice is over, except Artie, who just spent the entire time watching us from a bench. I don't think I've ever seen him look so miserable, but I get it. I think I'd be a grouch, too, if all I could do was watch my friends play a sport I love and not be able to take part myself.

Thankfully, his cast comes off at the end of the week, but he'll still have about another four weeks of physical therapy before he's able to play again. I know he's itching to get back on the court with us, and watching us practice all week is going to be pure hell, but he'll be joining us soon enough. His health is what is most important. If that means he needs to take extra time off, then that's what he'll have to do. Of course, he isn't going to like it if that turns out to be the case.

"I think you need to work on your speed," Artie chirps

when I make my way over to him. Brendon is busy talking with the coaches, which is something he has to do more often than the rest of us since he's the captain. "You were looking a little slow out there today. Or maybe it's just because you had googly eyes for Brendon." A mischievous grin is on his lips as he talks, letting me know he's joking.

"I'm the slow one?" I ask, looking at his cast then back at his face.

A look of pure shock spreads across his face before he bursts into laughter. "Fuck… That was… a good one." It takes him a moment before he can breathe fully and get himself under control, but I'm thankful that he's no longer moping. "But in all honesty, you all look amazing," he tells me once he can string together a full sentence without having to stop in between.

I sit beside him and clap him on the shoulder. "And you'll be just as good once you're able to join us," I remind him.

He nods, but his smile slips from his face. "Deep down, I know that. But missing so much time with the team is royally going to suck. You'll have already started to gel by the time I'm able to join, and I'm afraid Coach will want to bench me for most of the season."

"You're an amazing player, and missing a couple of games at the beginning of the season is not going to have Coach benching you," I assure him. "But what *will* fuck everything up is you pushing yourself too hard too soon. You need to take your time once you get out of that cast and listen to the physical therapists. Don't try to go balls to the wall. That will guarantee you a spot on the bench for the entire season. Not because you don't gel with us, but because you'll be injured."

Artie sighs but nods. "I know you're right, but it still fucking sucks."

"I know, but hey, maybe this will be your friendly reminder not to do stupid stuff to impress a girl."

My statement brings the light back to Artie's face, and the

corners of his lips turn up. "You'd think that would be the case, but I'm not too sure because my stupidity actually worked. Izzy is fucking amazing, and I'm not sure we'd be dating if it wasn't for me being an idiot."

I chuckle and shrug. "Well, now that you've got the girl, you shouldn't have to do any insane shit to get her attention anymore. As long as you don't fuck things up."

"Believe me. I don't plan on fucking this up," he assures me, and I believe him.

Izzy has been over to our place a few times now and it's easy to see they are both crazy about each other. I could see them being together for the long haul.

Just like Brendon helps balance me, Izzy does the same for Artie. Their personalities complement each other, and they really are the perfect match.

"Oh look, here comes your man," Artie says with a tip of his chin as Brendon saunters over to us.

"How are you doing?" Brendon asks Artie once he reaches us before taking a seat on the bench beside me.

I grab Brendon's hand then lean back so they can continue to talk.

"I'm okay," he replies with a shrug. "Sure hate just being a spectator, though."

"I totally understand that," Brendon tells him, knowing what our friend is going through from firsthand experience. "But you'll be on the court with us before you know it."

Artie nods. "I know. I just wish it was like today," he responds with a grin.

"You get the cast off Friday, right?" Brendon checks.

"Yup. And it can't come fast enough. Are you still able to drive me?"

Brendon nods. "That's the plan. And by then, Carter and I will have both our vehicles in working order."

"I still can't believe someone vandalized your car like that," Artie says to me, shaking his head.

Brendon squeezes my hand as if sensing that my anxiety is rising, and I shoot him a thankful glance.

"I can't believe it happened either," I respond, turning my attention back to him. "I just wish the cops would catch the guy already."

Artie is one of the few people who knows the full details about what's going on, and that's only because he lives with us and could possibly be caught in the crossfire of this crazy person.

"I'll keep my fingers crossed that they find whoever is doing this as soon as possible," he tells us.

"Thanks," I respond with a small smile.

We are going to need all the good vibes we can get because I've got this gut feeling that things are only going to escalate with this guy.

CHAPTER THIRTY

SINCE BRENDON TOOK Artie to the doctor after school, I'm on my own for dinner and decide to pick up some pizza, making sure to get enough so that there are leftovers for when the guys get home.

My hands are full of pizza boxes as I leave our favorite spot, and I almost run into someone who is walking down the street.

"Shit. I'm so sorry," I apologize, trying to make sure I don't drop the boxes.

"It's okay. I should have been paying more attention to where I was going," the man says, and I realize that it's Matais.

"It's totally okay. You're Matais, right?" I check with him, and he nods.

"That's me, and you're Carter?"

I smile at him. "Yup. Brendon told me a lot about you last year. You pretty much saved his ass with that assignment the two of you worked on."

He waves me off. "It was an easy assignment and Brendon was busy with basketball. It was the least I could do to take on the majority of the workload. Do you need help with those pizzas?" he asks, and I half shrug, half nod.

"Sure, if you don't mind, you can grab one if you'd like," I tell him, and he grabs one of the boxes from my hands and follows me to my car.

"You know, Carter, I really wish you'd have listened, then it wouldn't have come to this. This is really your own fault. So... sorry... not sorry," he murmurs, and before I can process what he's saying, I feel a sting in my neck.

Oh Shit! Matais is M! And... and...

But I can't think anymore. My head spins, making me stumble. The pizzas in my hands fall as numbness engulfs my whole body, washing over me like a tidal wave. Then I'm falling fast, prepared to hit the ground, but it doesn't come. My world goes dark.

"UGGGGHHHH," I groan out loud. It's the first thing I'm aware of as I slowly wake up with a splitting headache. "Fuck, B. What the hell did we drink?" I manage to force out between my dry lips. My mouth feels like it's the Sahara Desert; it puts a whole new spin on the term 'dry mouth', that's for sure.

My head is spinning, so I keep my eyes shut and just breathe while focusing on waking up. What the hell did we do last night? I don't remember much at all, and I'm starting to think that whatever it was, I won't want to do it again because this hangover is next level shitty.

"Yo, B! Do you feel as awful as me?" I croak out again in my half-awake state.

I go to reach out to him, but I can't move. All at once, memories crash their way back into my skull, making me reel and want to vomit. Bile rises up into the back of my throat, but with a concerted effort, I manage to push it back down. The acrid taste of it is left in my mouth, not making the dry-mouth situation any better.

I manage to peel my eyes open but am still left in the dark.

Shifting my weight around, I find that my ankles are bound together by rope that has been wound around and around them before being passed between my ankles and feet to bind the rope loops together. This creates thick manacles that are impossible to get out of without undoing the knots. My wrists are bound likewise behind my back, making undoing them hopeless.

Already, I'm struggling to keep my anxiety from over-whelming me, but I can feel the panic rising like a tsunami on the horizon. It's not here yet, but it will be.

"But it's not here yet," I whisper out loud. "What would B do?" I ask myself a little bit louder. My BFF turned boyfriend is the calmest and most logical guy I know while under pressure. It's one of the things that makes him an incredible team captain.

"Ok, ok... think... think... the basics. What basic information can I figure out?"

How about... Where the fuck am I? That's a good place to start.

It's completely dark wherever this is. I squirm around and can feel a slightly rough texture against my hands. I rub the side of one of my tied hands against it but quickly stop as the friction is chafing my skin. It's rug-burn! This must be a carpeting material of some kind. Well, that's something at least. But where?

I shuffle and squirm some more, then using the heel of my hand and as many fingers as I can, I push off hard, trying to sit up.

My head is barely a foot or so higher when it comes crashing into something hard and unforgiving. "Ahhh... what the..."

My whole body falls back down again, but this time, I've managed to land on my other side.

I'm clearly in a confined space of some kind. That's when I

see it. A small glow-in-the-dark square with an image of a car on it. I'm in the trunk of a car!

Matais, that shithead, has locked me in a fucking trunk! But why?

He must be the M from the note, and now he's fucking drugged and kidnapped me.

But what exactly does he plan to do with me? If he just wanted me out of the picture, he would have killed me already, but I'm still alive, which means he has more up his sleeve.

I need to get out of wherever I am now!

That's when I recall the glowing square. Like most people, M must not realize that all cars after a certain date have a safety release in the trunk. Now, I just need to find a way to press it.

I have no idea how long I try to find a way to push the damn button, but It feels like hours. Each passing moment has that tsunami of anxiety rising higher and higher. It's now of skyscraper proportions, and all at once it slams down on me.

I completely let go and fall into hysterics.

I scream and cry… sob and plead… a beg to be let out. I beg to live!

The terror is overwhelming me. I'm losing myself to it. I wish Brendon was here to hold me, to push back the darkness that threatens to overtake me. Brendon… My Brendon… B… my other half… my soul mate… my light in the darkness!

That's what he is. He's my flashlight, my security, my home, my lifeline.

He's my everything.

It's as simple as that. I don't know why I didn't see it before. It's almost too obvious. We've built our lives together and around each other; our lives have been so intertwined since we were little. Our refusal to have it any other way, even way back then, speaks volumes to the strength of our connection.

I need Brendon at this moment, and maybe he can help me, even if he's not here. I focus all my thoughts on him as I go through some breathing techniques to try and get myself together.

I think about all the times we played as children, all the trouble we used to get into together. I think about us first learning to play basketball and how quickly we both became obsessed. We'd spend hours and hours together playing in his driveway or mine, competing to see who could make more baskets while moving farther and farther back.

I think about high school, and more ball. Learning to perfect our jump-shots and lay-ups. Going on dates with girls and hating anytime either of us had a girlfriend because we'd see each other less.

It's working. I can feel the inner darkness that's been hovering all too close, being pushed back by my memories. I latch on to that fact and keep going.

I think about graduating and us both coming to GSU together. All the years of practices and games. Time spent together on and off the court. Our bi awakening and discovering just how deep our feelings for each other go. Holding him and being held. Connecting on a whole new level and the incredible feeling of rightness and finally being complete... of home. That's the exact word... home. Brendon is my home, just like I'm his.

Finally my heart rate slows, and my breathing becomes more even and deeper. I take a few minutes to hold myself mentally in the warmth of everything that is Brendon and me.

When I'm ready, I turn my thoughts back to the here and now but decide not to give into the panic this time —I can't. I have to be smarter. I have to survive this. I have to get back to the love of my life.

I think about Matais and all that I can remember about him from the stuff Brendon mentioned last year. He's a loner type, shy at first, but warmed up quickly once he was comfortable. Brendon has that effect on people. Even so, the guy was always the quiet type, a real brooder.

That must be when it happened. That must be when Matais first crushed on Brendon. But to him, Brendon was the unattainable, alpha male, sports God, who was straight. Somehow, he's learned that Brendon isn't as straight as he once thought.

That must be it. That's what is driving Matais. He has to think that he has a shot with him. If it weren't for me, that is.

Well, too damn bad, asshole. Brendon is mine, you fucker, and that's never going to change. My only hope is that Matais has more planned for me and that he's not left me to slowly die in this trunk.

Maybe the only reason I'm still alive right now is because Matais didn't want to kill me in town and has some other plan instead. As sick as it is, I have to hope for that option. Unfortunately, there's still a strong possibility that my death is imminent.

Hot tears trail down my cheeks as my chest tightens at the thought, but I quickly rein it in. I refuse to go down that path again. I need to stay calm. I need to focus so I can find a way forward. My only chance is going to be to try and use Matais' feelings against him. I'm not sure how yet, but I'll have to think on the fly.

I'm not sure how long it has been since I woke up, but it's been dead silent the entire time. Eerily so. I must be in the middle of nowhere so there isn't even use in screaming. I just have to wait to see what Matais is going to do with me.

I'm beginning to think he's just going to leave me in this trunk to rot when, all at once, three things happen in rapid succession. I hear the back passenger door open, the seat back behind me drops down, and a needle is jabbed into my butt cheek.

Damn it to hell. Not again!

CHAPTER THIRTY-ONE

WHEN ARTIE and I get home, I'm surprised to find the apartment empty.

"Where's Carter?" Artie asks, clearly just as confused as I am.

"Not a fucking clue," I murmur, pulling my phone out to see if he sent me a text that I somehow missed.

The last message he sent me was that he was getting pizzas and there would be leftovers when Artie and I got home. With quick steps I head to the fridge and frown when I don't find any pizzas. If there was a change of plans Carter would have told me, which makes me think maybe something else happened.

"We need to go for a drive," I tell Artie, who nods and follows me back to my car.

Once I'm behind the wheel, I pull up Carter's location and see that he's still at the pizza joint.

"Do you think someone slashed his tires again?" Artie asks as I speed down the streets.

I fucking hope that's all that's happened, but my gut is telling me something more sinister might have taken place. Carter would have told me something like that. The fact that he hasn't sent me any messages at all has me more than a little worried.

When we pull into the parking lot, I see Carter's car out front and park beside it, but my man isn't anywhere in sight.

Quickly I get out of the car and start to look around. The car is locked, but Carter's phone is on the passenger seat, which isn't like him. He always keeps it in his pocket.

My heart races as I stride toward the pizza joint and rush inside.

"Oh, hi, Brendon. Did Carter not pick up enough pizza?" Mary, the owner, asks.

And I shake my head. "So, he was here?" I check, and she nods.

"Yes, several hours ago. He picked up three large pizzas for you guys," she tells me, and I grab the back of my neck, trying to think what the hell happened and where he could possibly be.

"He didn't come home, and his car is still in the parking lot," I inform Mary, who gasps. "Did you see anyone else around when he picked up the pizzas?"

Mary shakes her head while frowning. "No, but I was pretty busy around then. A bunch of orders came in, and I was in the back making them up if there wasn't someone at the counter. So, there could have been someone outside that I just didn't notice. I can pull up my cameras, though, and see if they show anything," she suggests. "We actually just got them fixed a couple of days ago. They've been down for a while now, but this makes me extra thankful that my nephew was finally able to come down and help me out."

"That would be amazing. While you do that, I'm going to call the police."

"Absolutely, dear. Once you are off the phone with them, come right back to my office," she states before rushing away.

"What are you thinking happened?" Artie asks, and I shake my head.

"I have no idea, but I don't think it's anything good," I murmur while pulling my phone out.

Before I call the police I send Sasha a text, giving him a heads up about the situation and he immediately replies telling me he's on his way.

"Detective Leroy speaking," the officer who is running our case answers after I dial his number.

"Hi, it's Brendon. I'm at Deep Dish Delight, and I think Carter might have been kidnapped," I inform him, my hand shaking as I hold my phone to my ear.

"What makes you think that?" he asks, sounding so fucking calm when I feel anything but.

"The owner told us he picked up pizzas a few hours ago, but his car and cell phone are still here. She is pulling up the security footage for us now, but I know something happened. Carter isn't one to leave his phone behind, like ever, and where would he have taken the pizzas if he didn't get in his car?"

Detective Leroy hums in response before telling me he'll be here in a few minutes.

"Come on, let's see if Mary found anything," I tell Artie once I'm off the phone.

Even though I'm freaking out on the inside, I know I have to stay in control right now. Carter needs me, and letting my worry take over isn't going to help him.

"Come here," Mary waves us over when we enter her office. "Do you guys recognize this man?" she asks, hitting play.

The video shows Carter coming out of the store and bumping into someone. At first we can't see the face of the other person but eventually as they talk he turns, and I gasp when I realize who it is.

"That's Matais," I whisper, covering my mouth in disbelief.

As the video continues to play, he grabs one of the boxes of pizza and follows behind Carter until they are out of range of the camera.

"Do you have another angle?" I check, and she nods.

"My nephew installed another one the other day as well," she tells me, switching feeds.

We watch as Matais follows Carter to his car, and we all gasp when Matais injects something into Carter's neck, and my man goes limp, the pizza boxes falling to the ground.

Matais catches Carter and drags him to a car that is parked close by. With the way that the car is parked, they disappear from view around the back, and I can't tell what he's doing to Carter. About three minutes later, he appears again, cleans up the pizza, and locks Carter's phone in his car. After that, he gets in his car and drives off, making my blood run cold.

"I am so sorry this happened," Mary whispers, tears streaming down her face.

Gently I place my hand on her shoulder and give it a comforting squeeze. "This isn't your fault, and this footage gives us a lot to go off of," I tell her.

She nods. "I guess you're right. Do you think that person is going to hurt Carter?" she asks.

I shake my head. "I don't exactly know," I reply.

"Well, I'll keep you all in my thoughts, and if there is anything I can do, please let me know. Carter is a good kid, and so are the two of you," she tells us. I thank her before walking to the front of the store with Artie by my side.

"Don't give up hope, man," he encourages me as we step outside.

"I'm not," I assure him. "But we have no idea what Matais is capable of. It seems he wants me for himself, and I'm pretty sure he'll do anything to make that happen."

CHAPTER THIRTY-TWO

THIS TIME, when I come to, I'm not as groggy as before. He must have given me a lower dose than before.

Now, instead of being in the trunk, I'm tied to a chair in what I think is a run-down barn. The ropes are just as tight and well-constructed as the ones from before, but now, each ankle is tied to a chair leg. My hands are bound on the other side of the chair back, but also secured down to the chair itself as well. I can't help but pull against them, even though I know there is no getting loose. Matais knows his way around a rope.

Fucking great.

I try to keep the panic at bay, channeling my inner Brendon again, and begin to take in the space around me. There are a few gas lantern lights hung up around the place, a small table a few feet away from me, and a raggedy old couch near it. The place is pretty dimly lit but there is just enough for me to see around clearly.

The air is filled with a musty odor, and when I look up, there are holes in the roof, letting me see the night sky in bits and pieces.

What time is it? When I was in the trunk, it felt like I must have been there all night, but clearly, there's still some night left. I must not have been sedated as long as I thought I had, but just how long have I been gone?

"Ah, you're finally awake," Matais says as he walks into the barn, his shoes scuffing against the dirt floor.

"Why did you take me?" I ask him, needing to try and get some answers and figure out how best to play this.

"Because you were in my way," he replies nonchalantly. "I'm still trying to figure out what exactly to do with you, though."

"You could just let me go," I suggest. "I won't tell anyone you took me."

"Would you stay away from Brendon?" he asks with a tilt of his head.

A small glimmer of hope bubbles up inside of me, and I bobble my head, praying he'll believe the lie I'm about to spew. "If that's what you want, I promise I will."

Matais throws his head back as he laughs, stealing away any idea I'd had that he might be stupidly obsessed, emphasis on stupid. The type of obsessed that loses all rational thinking. Too bad, that would have made him a lot easier to manipulate.

"Do you really think I'm that stupid to believe a lie like that?"

Slowly, he steps towards me, and the glint of something in his hand pulls my attention. Fuck. He's holding a giant hunting knife. What the hell is he going to do with that?

"I know I'm going to have to get rid of you. I just haven't figured out how quite yet. But once you are out of the picture, I'll have Brendon all to myself."

I try to keep my breathing even, knowing I can't let the panic take over again. Not if I want to get out of this. I need to probe further; see which way to take this.

"You took me in a public place, Matais. Do you really think no one saw?" I check. "The cops are going to figure out you were the one behind all of this, and you're going to get arrested. Brendon will never love you, especially if you hurt me, but if you let me go now, I'll make a statement on your behalf. You can get help, and you won't have to spend the rest of your life in prison."

"Shut up!" he yells in my face, his spittle hitting my nose and making me shudder. "You don't know anything."

Shit. I shouldn't have poked the bear. The knife shakes in his grip, and I lean back as much as I can, pressing my lips together and praying that he doesn't cut me. My anxiety is threatening to take over my body, as it normally does when I'm frightened, but I can't let it have control. I need to stay as calm as possible if I'm going to get out of this situation alive.

"There was no one around when I grabbed you, and Deep Dish Delight's cameras have been down for months. I know this because someone stole my bike a couple of weeks ago, and they couldn't help me," he informs me, making my stomach curdle. "Brendon will never find out I was the one that made you disappear, and once he's done grieving, I'll be the one he falls for. I'll make sure of it."

I need to come up with a fucking plan to keep this fucked up psycho from killing me right now.

Suddenly, an idea hits me, and I spit out words that feel beyond wrong to say. "What if he already loves you and just doesn't realize it?" I ask, making Matais take a step back.

"What do you mean?" he questions with a tilt of his head, studying me intently.

"Well, you only signed the note from M, not Matais, so he doesn't know it's you that loves him. What if you told him the truth? He already can tell how well you know him and how much you care, maybe all he needs is to know it's you.

Brendon and I are mostly just exploring things, and if he's actually crazy about you, I'd gladly walk away. You know that we're best friends. All I want is for him to be happy. Everything can go back to normal. You just have to tell him the truth."

He paces as he thinks about what I said.

I know that there is no way Brendon would ever love him,

but if I can convince Matais otherwise, and he makes the call, maybe that will help me get rescued. That's really my only way forward right about now. It's the only hope I have to cling to, and if I let go of it, my anxiety will take over, and I'm as good as dead.

"Don't you think it's worth the shot?" I prod him, needing him to believe this web of lies I'm spinning. "You don't even have to tell him I'm here. Just tell him you love him."

The knife shakes by his side as he walks back and forth across the dirt floor. He moves his free hand up to run it through his hair, and I know he's considering doing what I'm telling him to.

I'm not sure how long he shuffles along, but eventually, he marches over to one end of the barn and starts to rifle through a bag.

"If I'm going to do this, I have to make sure you don't make a fucking sound," he says as he stalks over to me, a roll of duct tape in his hand.

I'd argue with him, but I know it would be a moot point, so I allow him to seal my lips closed.

All I can do is pray that Brendon knows that I'm missing and realizes Matais is the one who took me when he gets the call.

CHAPTER THIRTY-THREE

Brendon

DETECTIVE LEROY and his partner showed up at Deep Dish Delight about twenty minutes after my call and immediately started asking me a bunch of questions that had my head spinning. I know that they are just trying to get as much information as possible, but time is of the essence, and they need to track down Matais now. I need Carter in my arms as soon as possible.

Right now, the officers are watching the security footage and I'm hanging out with Sasha and Artie, trying not to go crazy. And I'm really trying not to think about the worst-case scenario. If I let my thoughts go down that trail there will be no bringing me back.

My phone buzzes in my pocket, and when I pull it out, I damn near drop it as my eyes see the name on the screen.

I race to the office where the officers are and tell them who's calling.

"Answer it on speaker phone, and we'll be quiet," Detective Leroy tells me. "Do more listening than talking. Do not let him know that we are onto him."

I nod and swipe open the call.

"Hello?" I answer, trying to keep my voice from shaking.

"Hey, Brendon, I hope it's okay that I called," he says in such a sweet voice that it's almost hard to believe that he's the one behind all this shit that's been happening.

"Absolutely," I reply, keeping my response short to give him more time to talk like the detective told me to do.

"I kind of wanted to tell you something," he informs me after a brief pause.

"What's that?" I check, my entire body shaking.

"I'm the one who sent you that gift basket," he confesses. "I know I went about things wrong, but I'm crazy about you, and I keep kicking myself for not telling you sooner. I just thought you were straight and that I didn't have a chance. Maybe if I had just told you, you would have realized that you liked guys sooner. I know you're with Carter right now, but I was hoping maybe I meant as much to you as you do to me and that you and I could give things a try."

Detective Leroy nods at me and quickly scribbles down on a notebook for me to agree with Matais and ask if he knows where Carter is.

"Oh wow," I respond, trying to come up with something to say that sounds believable. "I had no idea you had feelings for me, but I can tell you really get me from just how thoughtful that gift basket was. I've always thought you were a really great guy, and now that I think about it, I'm pretty sure I had a crush on you," I lie, bile rising up my throat and threatening to make me gag.

"Really?" he questions, sounding hopeful but doubtful at the same time.

"Yeah. I just figured out I was bi when I got back to school, and I think I just jumped into things with Carter because he was there. But looking back, I realize I was totally into you. I just couldn't see it because I thought I was straight." My stomach curdles as the lies roll off my lips.

"That actually makes a lot of sense," he murmurs. Thankfully he's buying the bullshit I'm selling. "Does that mean you're willing to give us a shot?" he checks, hope filling his voice.

"Umm yeah, I think that's a great idea. But I'll have to let

Carter down gently. That is once I find him. I've been trying to get a hold of him all night, but he's kind of disappeared."

"Oh, he's actually with me. We ran into each other at Deep Dish Delight, and he forgot his phone in the car," Matais says like it's no big deal, but I know it's a lie. "He's actually the one who encouraged me to call you. He agrees that you and I make a better pair."

Detective Leroy scribbles down a note telling me to get their location.

"Oh, that's cool," I respond. "Why don't you send me your location? I'll come out there. Carter can take my car home, and you and I can spend some time together."

"Umm yeah, that sounds good," he murmurs. "We're hanging out on my grandpa's property right now. He's got an old barn that I use when I want to get away from the city."

"Sounds good to me. Just drop me your location," I encourage him.

"Okay, see you soon," he tells me and ends the call.

Immediately, I rush to the corner where the garbage can is and vomit what little is in my stomach, followed by dry heaving as my body rebels against the poison I had to spew out to such a vile creature. When I'm done, Sasha has a damp paper towel to wipe my mouth with and a glass of water. I wipe first, then take a few small sips, grateful to have something to wash the taste out of my mouth.

I put the glass down on the desk and check my phone, there's a message waiting with his location on my screen. All I want to do is rush to my man's rescue then hold him tight and never let go. I feel like I'd run the risk of becoming a stage five clinger, but I'm absolutely ok with that.

I show the message to the officer. "I'll dispatch units to that location now," Detective Leroy tells me, but I shake my head.

"You can't do that," I growl out. "Matais is expecting me

and only me. What if he kills Carter when the cops show up and I'm not there?"

Detective Leroy shoots his partner a look which only pisses me off more.

"I'm not saying I have to go in on my own, but I do have to show up first. I will not have you or anyone else put Carter's life at risk."

"The kid's not wrong," his partner states. "We can radio in our information, get back up on route, and tail him from a safe distance."

Detective Leroy purses his lips and huffs out a breath. "Fine, but don't do anything stupid," he commands, pointing his finger at me. "The situation needs to be as calm as possible. Don't do anything to rile Matais up. Keep his attention on you while we get into position. We'll enter as soon as we are sure that you and Carter aren't in immediate danger." I nod and make a move to leave the office, but Detective Leroy grabs my arm, stopping me. "I also want you to wear a bullet-proof vest, just in case."

A lump forms in my throat, and I swallow it down as I move my head up and down.

"Can we go now?" I check, feeling restless and needing to leave as soon as possible.

"Let me just radio in the details," he responds. "Meet me at my car to get that vest."

"Okay," I whisper before rushing to my friends to let them know what's going on.

"Please tell me Carter is okay," Sasha says when I get over to him.

"I honestly don't know," I reply. "But Matais says he is. I'm going to where he is now, and the detectives are following me, along with back up."

"This is fucking crazy," Artie murmurs.

"Would you mind giving Artie a ride home?" I ask Sasha.

"Of course. But are you sure you don't want us to go with you?" he asks, and I quickly shake my head.

"Absolutely not," I reply quickly. "I need to go by myself. If anyone else is with me, it might set Matais off, and I will not put Carter at risk."

Artie and Sasha nod.

"We understand. Just be safe," Artie tells me.

"I'll do my best," I assure him, not making any promises I can't keep.

In the end, I would sacrifice myself to rescue Carter. I'd do it in a heartbeat, not even thinking twice. And It's not just because he's in this mess because of his relationship with me. It's because I love him more than my own life. More than anything else in the entire world.

I can't even imagine a life where Carter isn't there right beside me, and I refuse to ever try. They both pat me on the back before taking off, and I head to the parking lot and wait for Detective Leroy.

Needing to pump myself up for this, I center my thoughts.

Failure is not an option.

Losing Carter is not an option.

I will go in there and lie and charm my way into getting Carter out.

I will say anything that I have to, to get my man back.

If I have to pretend to say the things I'd only ever mean to Carter, then I will.

I am not going to let this scumbag ruin what Carter and I have together.

He doesn't get to decide who I can and can't love or be with.

I'm going to go in there, fake my way through an Oscar-worthy performance,

And damn well get my man… back!

Now I'm pumped and ready to get moving. I'm so close to being with my man I can fucking taste it.

CHAPTER THIRTY-FOUR

MATAIS COMES BACK into the barn with a giant smile on his face, which must mean that he was successful. It also has to mean that Brendon has to know that I've been kidnapped, and Matais is the one who's taken me. Although that fact is comforting, it still doesn't do much to ease my nerves. There are so many possibilities for whatever Brendon has planned and so many ways that it all could still go to shit.

But I've gotta believe that it will all go well, or I'm going to lose my mind. Thankfully, I'm still channeling my inner Brendon, so I'm still somehow keeping hold of my anxiety. That, and I just keep thinking about Brendon and spending the rest of my life with him. I have got to get out of this alive, and the only way that's going to happen is by keeping my composure.

"You were right," he tells me, sauntering my way with a swagger to his step — it's sickening. "Brendon does love me, and he's coming to be with me." He tears the tape off my lips so quickly that it burns, and I can't help but wince.

Matais reaches behind his back and unsheathes that damn hunting knife again. He twirls it in his hand before bringing it up to my face, right beside the outside of my eye. I desperately want to pull against the ropes that bind me, but I'm afraid that any slight movement will have me bleeding.

Slowly he drags the tip of it down my face, I can tell how

sharp it is, because it lightly scratches, even though there is only a whisper of pressure being used.

"Now you just have to tell him that we ran into each other, and you lost track of time. Do you think you can do that, Carter?" He asks as he taps the flat of the blade against my cheek.

I slowly nod.

"Good, because if you tell him the truth, I won't hesitate to kill you." His tone is menacing and leaves no room for argument.

I know I have to agree with him, but I really wish I knew what Brendon has planned. I'm sure my man is rushing his way towards us. I just hope he isn't stupidly coming without proper backup. "I won't tell him," I assure him. "I'm happy for the two of you."

Matais rolls his eyes. "You're a terrible liar."

Crap, I have to sell this better. I know I'm a shit liar, so I'll have to go with something true. "Ok, so happy isn't the right word. What I meant was that Brendon and I have been best friends all our lives, and all I want is for *him* to be happy. If he's decided that isn't with me, then I'm ok with that."

Matais stares at me, watching me closely for a few moments. "I think you really mean that," he finally says.

"I do mean it," which is actually true. But I also know that Brendon doesn't want anyone else other than me. But it's not like I'm going to tell him that.

"Good because Brendon and I are going to be together now, and that's what matters."

He walks around behind me and squats down. "I'm going to cut you free now, and you're not going to do anything stupid." He says before suddenly the blade is at my throat. "Because if you do, I won't think twice about ending your life and staging it as an accident." The knife leaves my neck and is somewhere behind me.

"Brendon might not be in love with you, but you still

mean something to him. It would be a shame to actually have to kill you. Besides, you wouldn't want to bring him the kind of agony that seeing your dead body would."

"No," I whisper and take a shaky breath. "I promise I'll behave."

He lets out an unhinged laugh while starting to cut through the ropes. "I know you will."

Once my limbs are loose, I move my arms to my sides and roll my shoulders trying to get the circulation to flow again and regain some feeling.

"Go sit on the couch and have some pizza," Matais commands, and I don't fight him.

I need to regain my strength, and food will help me do that. Matais isn't a big guy and definitely isn't as strong or as fast as me, but right now, I wouldn't be able to fight him if I needed to. So, I'm going to take this opportunity to rest, eat, and try to mentally come up with options on how to handle whatever plan B has.

"There's water in that cooler, too," he tells me with a smile, pointing to the small ice chest by the couch.

I pull out a bottle and guzzle down the contents before grabbing a slice of pizza and devouring it.

Matais is now being too nice to me, and it's making me even more uneasy. I know he has ulterior motives and wants to get on Brendon's good side, but I can't help but feel the other shoe is about to drop.

He's too happy right now. What happens if things don't go according to his fucked-up plans when Brendon arrives? Is he going to try and kill all of us?

I'm on my third slice of pizza and halfway through a second bottle of water when I hear tires over gravel getting closer.

"He's here," Matais says, beaming at the entrance of the barn.

He grabs the knife he's been twirling between his fingers

and slides it into a sheath that I can now see is on his belt at the back of his pants. "Remember to stick to the script, or shit is going to go sideways," he hisses out between his teeth with a slight snarl.

I nod, not wanting to piss him off because I really don't know what he's capable of.

Matais makes his way to the barn door, and I stay firmly in place, afraid to move just yet.

"Sorry I took so long," Brendon says as he walks into the barn. Matais beams at him like he hung the moon.

Brendon's eyes land directly on mine, and he stares at me for a moment, silently asking if I'm okay.

I dip my chin, letting him know I'm fine, for the moment anyway.

"It's okay," Matais tells Brendon. "I'm just glad you're here."

Brendon plasters on a fake smile when he looks at Matais and it makes me feel better and want to puke at the same time. It's good that I know how fake this is for B, but I hate that we have to put on this act at all. But it's certainly better than either of us dying. That means we have to do what we have to do right now.

"Hey, C," Brendon tells me, making his way toward the couch that I'm sitting on with Matais directly beside him. I stand up, and he reaches his hand out to me. Taking it, he pulls me in for a typical back-slapping bro-hug that we'd give any one of our friends. Between us, though, he squeezes my hand tight just as I squeeze his back. This small hidden gesture is our real selves. It's the comfort and assurance that we both need in this moment. It's over too fast.

Moving his body away from mine, his left hand goes to the side of my shoulder but still keeps the handshake. Here we go. Here come the lies, and we both have to sell it.

"I'm glad you see things clearly. We both want what's best for each other, right?" he says. The dual meaning is clear to only me because we both know that what's best for us is to be together, always.

"Of course, B," I get out, a bit more forced sounding than is entirely safe. So, I clear my throat while Brendon continues on, to help cover my emotions.

"I think Matais and I could be good together. Enough that I have to give this a real try."

Tears start to fill my eyes, but I force myself to push them away. I know it's a lie, and only said to protect me, but the words still sting.

"I just want you to be happy," I respond, trying to keep my voice as even as possible.

"Thanks, C. Here are the keys to my car. You should take off," he says, reaching his hand out and placing them in mine. "Matais will give me a ride home later."

My brows pinch together as I try to figure out just what Brendon's plan is. The last thing I want to do is leave him alone with this crazy person.

"That's okay with you, right?" Matais asks, wrapping one hand around Brendon's side and reaching the other around his back, reminding me of the knife.

Bile rises up my throat, but I force myself to nod.

"Yeah. That's fine with me," I tell them and take a step to the side.

I'm about to walk out when the tell-tale crunch of gravel echoes outside the barn.

"Is someone else here?" Matais asks, looking at Brendon with wide eyes.

"No," Brendon says, trying to calm Matais down. "It's just me. That was probably an animal."

Matais shakes his head as he pulls out his knife. "You're lying to me," he shouts, pointing the weapon at Brendon's chest.

"It was probably just an animal," I assure Matais, taking a step toward the barn door and peering out. My eyes land on

Detective Leroy, who is holding his finger up to his lips, silently telling me not to say anything. My entire body is on edge, but I try to keep myself as calm as possible when I turn back around and move a few steps back into the room. "I don't see any other vehicles out there, and you saw Brendon arrive alone."

Matais' hand shakes as he turns his head back and forth. "I don't know what I believe," he mutters, raising his hands to pull on his hair as he takes a step back.

"It's just me," Brendon assures him before turning to look at me. "You can go, C," he says to me, but Matais shouts, "No!"

"No one is leaving. I know you're lying," he yells at Brendon, who's quickly moved towards me, meeting in the middle of the room. "Why can't you love me? Why am I never good enough for anyone?" Matais screams.

"That's enough, Matais," Detective Leroy shouts, walking into the barn with his gun drawn. "Drop the knife."

Matais' entire body is shaking as he mutters, "No... no... no," over and over again. "No. If I can't have him, no one can," he yells before grabbing one of the gas lanterns and throwing it at the base of a large pile of loose hay beside the barn entrance. The glass smashes, exposing the naked flame to the waiting pile of tinder. Instantly, the pile lights, and in the next breath, the flame climbs up and spreads across the side towards both the barn roof and wall.

Detective Leroy jumps out of the way of the fire that is now quickly engulfing the run-down structure. Brendon and I are both so distracted that neither of us notice Matais until it's too late. I'm pulled back by a surprisingly strong grip around my waist and feel the tip of that big knife digging into the side of my back.

"This is all your fault." He snarls out in a shout that can be heard over the rising sounds of the fire that is quickly spreading. "You stole the man I love from me. You don't get to be happy. You don't get to walk away from this. I'd rather be dead than watch either of you happy, so I'm going to take you all with me."

A loud peel of a gunshot going off rings out, so deafening that it stuns me for a moment. But then the grip Matais has on me slackens and releases as he falls to the ground. I turn and look down, seeing a lifeless expression on his face as blood oozes out of his head.

"Over there, let's go!" Detective Leroy shouts, pulling my attention away from Matais' dead body.

He's pointing to a hole in the back wall. Still stunned, I don't register his meaning right away. Brendon takes action and grabs my hand to pull me toward it. I stumble, my body still weak from exhaustion and the remains of whatever Matais drugged me with, but thankfully, my man still has all his strength and pulls me tight into his side, supporting me as we move to the small opening. Using his powerfully muscular legs, he kicks at the boards over and over, breaking the wood to make the hole wide enough for us to exit.

The air around us has filled with smoke, making us all choke and cough, and the heat of the fire is rapidly becoming blisteringly hot as the building fills with flames.

Once the hole is big enough, Brendon drags me out, and Detective Leroy follows directly behind us.

Another officer sees us come through, approaches us quickly, and guides us away from the burning building.

"The ambulance is already here, and firetrucks are on their way," he tells us as we continue to cough and try desperately to take in deep breaths of fresh air.

As I try to take in another breath, my body decides it can't hold me up anymore, and I collapse to the ground.

"Get the EMTs over here now," Detective Leroy shouts, and Brendon pulls me into his arms.

"You came for me. I knew you would," I whisper, as I look into his eyes.

"Was there ever a possibility that I wouldn't?" he asks with a tilt of his head. "It's always been me and you against the world, and I would never let anyone take you from me," he assures me before leaning down to press his lips to mine.

I melt into his touch and almost want to yell at the paramedics when they arrive and make Brendon let me go.

"I'm not going anywhere, baby," he promises me as he moves out of their way but still holds my hand. It's something I'm grateful for and makes me clutch it that much harder.

I smile at him as they take my vitals and put an oxygen mask on my face.

I might be covered in dirt and ash and still have the remnants of an unknown drug in my system, but I also have the love of my life by my side, and that makes everything okay. We are alive, and we're together. Nothing else matters.

CHAPTER
THIRTY-FIVE

Brendon

I'M in between the realm of being awake and asleep when I hear the voice I love more than words can express.

"You don't look very comfortable," Carter tells me, bringing a soft smile to my lips.

I stretch my arms above my head and open my eyes, taking in the sight of my man in a hospital bed.

Carter is going to be fine, but the doctor wanted to observe him for several hours just to make sure. Seeing as we arrived at the hospital in the middle of the night, he decided it would be best for us to stay until morning.

"Sleeping in a chair sucks, but there was no way I was going to leave you," I tell him, making the corners of his lips turn upward.

"I appreciate the company, but I would have been fine on my own," he murmurs, and I shake my head.

"After everything you went through tonight, the last thing I wanted to do was be away from you. I'm so sorry Matais did all of this."

My throat fills with emotion, and tears fill my eyes as the guilt eats at me.

"None of this is your fault. You couldn't have known that Matais was secretly in love with you and that seeing us together would cause him to lose it," he reminds me.

"I know that deep down, but it doesn't stop these feelings from eating at me," I tell him.

"Well, it's a good thing we have the rest of our lives together. That way, I can remind you every day that none of this was your fault and that I love you more than words can say," he states with a smirk.

I lean forward and reach for his hand. "I love you so fucking much, C, and I'm really glad he didn't take you away from me."

"Me too," he replies quietly, squeezing my hand.

IT'S a couple more hours before the doctor makes his rounds and signs off on Carter's release. Both of us are beyond exhausted by the time we make it back home.

"You know we're going to have to tell our parents about last night at some point," Carter murmurs as we walk through the door of our apartment.

"We can do that and everything else —later, *after* a nap," I tell him as I pull him to my room.

We haven't told our parents about any of the crazy stuff that has been happening because we didn't want them to overreact, but now that everything is behind us, we definitely have to come clean. They are going to be pissed that we kept them in the dark, but they'll get over it eventually.

"Come on, handsome," I say to Carter as I pull the covers back. "I need you in my arms."

He beams at me before climbing in.

Once we are both under the covers, I pull my man into my arms, and he rests his head on my chest.

"This is where you belong," I whisper in a sleepy voice.

"Nowhere else I'd rather be," he replies, sounding just as tired.

Quickly, sleep pulls us under, and a feeling of pure contentment washes over me. Matais might have wanted to take me away from Carter, but there was never any chance of that happening willingly. My heart has always belonged to my best friend, and no one in this world could ever change that.

Carter is the only person I'll ever love. From now until forever.

The End

Thank you so much for reading Winning the Point Guard! If you loved this story please <u>leave an honest review!</u>

Up next we have Monster and Finn in - Challenging the Shortstop: *an m/m college baseball romance.*

Available now on Amazon and Kindle Unlimited. <u>Download Today.</u>

ALSO BY LAURA JOHN

*** Indicates M/M romance

GSU - M/M COLLEGE SPORTS SERIES

1. Schooling the Quarterback: (An M/M Tutor/Athlete Football Romance) ***

2. Testing the Goalie: (An M/M Professor/Student Hockey Romance) ***

3. Teasing the Winger: (An M/M Annoyances to Lovers Soccer Romance) ***

4. Winning the Point Guard: (An M/M, friends to lovers, bi-awakening, basketball romance) ***

5. Challenging the Shortstop: (An M/M baseball romance) ***

6. Pinning the Wrestler: (An M/M, ex's dad, wrestling romance)***

HUNTER SECURITY SERIES

1. Nixon: (An m/m bodyguard romance) ***

2. Denver: (An m/m best friends to lovers, single dad, bodyguard romance) ***

3. Knox: (A Suspenseful M/M Brother's Best Friend Romance) ***

4. Bennett: (An m/m bodyguard romance) ***

SULTRY SUMMER SERIES

1. Summer Heat (A FREE small town romance short story)

2. Long Summer Nights (A Small town low angst romance)

3. Summer Daze (A Small Town Interracial romance)

4. Summer Memories (A M/M second chance small town romance)***

5. Summer Dreams (A M/M Age Gap romance)***

LOVE IN SIENNA SERIES

1. Secret Smiles (A friends to lovers rock star romance) *ALSO AVAILABLE IN AUDIO!*

2. Hidden Kisses (An enemies to lovers baseball romance)

3. Guarded Hearts (A New adult, best friends to lovers, single mother romance.

4. Whispered Desires (A single mother, enemies to lovers, age gap, rock star romance)

5. Confidential Moments (A M/M Baseball romance)***

6. Clean Slates (A fast burn rock star romance)

7. Tangled Love (A rock star romance love triangle romance)

8. Restless Beat (A rock star romance)

9. Love In Sienna Boxset (Books 1-4)

10. Love in Sienna Boxset (Books 5-8)

SENTINEL PROTECTION DUOLOGY

1. Fighting Attraction (A M/M bodyguard romance)***

2. Embracing Temptation (A M/M age gap bodyguard romance)***

STANDALONES

Monster In The Shadows (Dark romance standalone)

Kissing in the snow (A M/M Christmas Novella set in the Sentinel Protection World)***

Afterglow (A kinky brother's best friend romance)

ACKNOWLEDGMENTS

Thank you so much for reading Winning the Point Guard. I truly hope you loved reading it!

Now onto the thank you's. There are always so many people to thank and I really hope I don't miss anyone. (But if I do I'm sorry.)

First and foremost, I want to thank my amazing team. I wouldn't be able to do any of this without them. They pick me up when I'm down and always have my back. Even though we have a business arrangement I consider them more friends than anything else. They are the hardest working women I have ever met and I am never going to let them go. So give it up for the women I couldn't live without, Brittany Franks and Suzanne Talkington!

Secondly, I want to thank my superb Alpha/Beta Readers Mandy, Robin, Shannon and Mentoah. These ladies are always pointing out the beginning issues and are always available for me to bounce ideas off of. I'd probably still be stuck trying to figure things out if it wasn't for them.

Next, my sensitivity readers for making sure that Brendon and Carter were portrayed properly. Darryl Bailey is a new friend to me but he was amazing to work with! He made sure that the m/m aspects of this book were on point and he did a fantastic job. Crystal helped with the bipoc aspect of the book and killed it as usually. Crystal is a joy to work with and I can't wait to use her again! Also Crystal helped me with proofreading this book and was able to catch those last minute pesky errors.

Next I want to thank my AMAZING new editor BreathlessLit. They were GREAT to work with and helped me polish this book and make it as strong as it is today.

Brittany Franks deserves her own place in the thank you's

because she is just that amazing. She absolutely blew me away with this cover! Brittany is a one of a kind person and I am beyond lucky to have found her and claim her as one of my friends. She is simply the best person in the entire world. Not only is she immensely talented but she's also genuinely the most caring person I have ever met. I truly love this woman with all my heart and am NEVER letting her go.

My family for putting up with me when I put myself on a deadline and go a little crazy.

And last but obviously not least... you... the reader... without you I wouldn't be continuing to put books out! Thank you for your continued support. I love you all so much!

ABOUT THE AUTHOR

Laura John is a steamy romance author from Alberta, Canada, who melds love and angst together while normalizing mental illness. She also brings a mixture of m/m and m/f books because love is love. In her books, you will fall in love with so many different book boyfriends it's not even funny! She really has something for everyone!

When she's not writing, she enjoys reading, going to concerts, hiking, and experimenting with makeup!

If you love connecting with authors and like minded readers join Laura's Readers group!

There are a lot more books coming soon so make sure to sign up for Laura's newsletter to stay up to date on everything!

www.ingramcontent.com/pod-product-compliance
Lightning Source LLC
Chambersburg PA
CBHW022144240626
47153CB00007B/2497